CLAIMING HIS
UNKNOWN SON

CLAIMING HIS UNKNOWN SON

KIM LAWRENCE

MILLS & BOON

First published in Great Britain 2020
by Mills & Boon, an imprint of HarperCollins*Publishers*
1 London Bridge Street, London, SE1 9GF

Large Print edition 2020

© 2020 Kim Lawrence

ISBN: 978-0-263-08512-9

MIX
Paper from
responsible sources
FSC **FSC C007454**
www.fsc.org

This book is produced from independently certified
FSC™ paper to ensure responsible forest management. For
more information visit www.harpercollins.co.uk/green.

Printed and bound in Great Britain
by CPI Group (UK) Ltd, Croydon, CR0 4YY

CHAPTER ONE

'No!'

The Madrigal Hotel's assistant manager was a consummate professional accustomed to the idiosyncrasies of the rich and famous so his practised smile stayed painted in place, despite the sudden outburst from the woman in front of him. He was rarely surprised, but at that moment, as he braced himself for a diva meltdown, he was.

He prided himself on being able to tell at first glance which of their VIP guests were going to be hard work, but he hadn't had this beautiful guest down as one of the awkward ones.

First impressions had certainly not given him any clues, as up to this point she had lived up to her public image. Her arrival had been low-key, as befitting the rarity she was said to be, someone not in the business of promoting *herself*, just good causes. People spoke about how freely she gave of her time and energy and her dedication in continuing to support the charities that she said were her late husband's legacy.

The rare unfriendly pieces that appeared in the media he had always attributed to the hack's frustration in not being able to find a story. You could see it from their point of view—they were used to being invited into the homes of the rich and famous, and Marisa Rayner never even gave them a glimpse behind closed doors.

There was still no meltdown forthcoming, but what was happening was even more alarming than a hissy fit. She hadn't moved a muscle; she was just standing there like a pale frozen statue. What if she was ill?

He experienced a sudden flurry of panic as the question entered his thoughts, realising that would also explain the other-worldly, almost unfocused expression in her wide amber eyes when she'd removed her fashionable shades earlier, as he'd walked beside her through the hotel's famous art deco doors. At the time he had put her pallor down to the lights from the glittering chandeliers overhead.

An ill guest was never good, but then he reasoned nobody who felt really ill would make such an effort to smile at all the staff she had encountered. At least, she had up until now.

The friendly, genuinely warm smile that charmed everyone it was aimed at was now totally absent as she stood on the threshold of one of their premiere suites looking as if she had seen a ghost.

He gave a philosophical shrug and waited. The Madrigal's reputation had been built in part on the hotel's ability to satisfy the most difficult of guests, especially when they had the money to pay the exorbitant prices the Madrigal charged for their premier luxury suites, and the lovely Marisa Rayner was one guest who could certainly afford it.

The fact she had been the sole beneficiary of her husband's considerable estate after his death made her a natural target of envy. The story of the rich older man married to a very much younger woman was a magnet for the scandal-loving red tops. She could have gone through her life with a 'gold-digger' label attached to her, but the forensic dirt-digging exercises had come up empty-handed and she was considered a scandal-free zone—aside from a little guilt by association. But even her dead father, with his colourful history of affairs and a taste for high-stakes gambling, was nothing in this day and age.

No young lovers pre- or post-marriage—just a few malicious suggestions, which was par for the course, but they had faded away too after she had not morphed as predicted into a 'merry widow', but had remained a dedicated, hard-working one devoted to charitable works.

The adjective mostly attached to her name was *classy* and for once, he decided, the press had it right.

If she had any skeletons in her closet they were deeply hidden.

'Do you have another room?' Marisa heard the quiver in her voice that stopped *just* the right side of hysteria, and bit down on her full lower lip while buying time to regain her composure by making a meal of smoothing back non-existent loose strands of shiny silver-blonde hair that was safely secured in a smooth simple knot on the nape of her swanlike neck.

She knew she had to pull herself together,

but unfortunately *knowing* that was no help right now.

'Another room? This is one of our—'

'Sorry, yes, this is marvellous,' she gushed. 'But…something…on a lower floor, perhaps? I… I don't have a very good head for heights.'

'Of course, if you'll just bear with me for a moment.' The man pulled out a slim tablet and began to scroll through it.

Get a grip, Marisa, she told herself fiercely, if for no other reason than this poor man who was only doing his job looked as if he wanted to run for the hills—and who could blame him? *Scared of heights?* She was beyond feeling embarrassed, no doubt that would come later when she revisited this moment—*in her nightmares!*

The gut-freezing panic had hit her the moment the taxi drew up outside the hotel. The signage on the well-known art deco frontage was ultra-discreet—it didn't need to be flashy; everyone knew the iconic façade of the Madrigal—but to Marisa those letters had seemed to be written in neon and came accompanied by a loud soundtrack of guilt and shame. She still couldn't remember how she had got out of the taxi, as the sheer horror of the moment had blanked her brain completely.

Of course it ought not to have been a shock, *wouldn't* have if she'd been paying attention. Her delicate dark blonde brows drew together in a straight line above her heavily lashed amber eyes. Even distracted, she had managed to hide her disappointment when her assistant, Jennie, had triumphantly announced that she'd managed the impossible and secured an alternative last-minute venue after their original booking at a country-house hotel had fallen through.

She could remember Jennie mentioning the prestige of the alternative venue, she *had* to have mentioned the name, but Marisa's mind had been elsewhere and she hadn't registered it. No, because she'd been too busy torturing herself with every possible, and highly improbable, disaster that could occur in her absence.

Her glance darted around the room, reached the slightly open bedroom door and retracted hastily, focusing instead on her feet clad in leg-elongating nude court shoes that added four inches to her willowy five feet ten inches.

She brought her lashes down in a protective sweep over eyes that continued to be drawn to that open door, her mouth twisted in frustration as she acknowledged all the missed opportunities that would have at least given her time, if not to avoid this moment, then to at the very least prepare herself for it.

Even as late as getting in the taxi would have been something, she thought, considering another missed opportunity. Jennie had waited until she was in the cab before they'd parted company, her PA heading towards the Tube to spend some well-deserved time off with her family. Jennie *had* to have given the driver the address of the hotel, but again Marisa's thoughts had been elsewhere.

Where was a convenient icy shiver of premonition when a girl needed one?

Up to the point the taxi had pulled in, she hadn't even glanced out of the window. Instead, she had spent the journey from the station scrolling through some emails and checking in with Jamie's nanny, Ashley, who had responded to her anxious questions with cheery positivity and a series of soothing photos of Marisa's four-and-a-half-year-old clearly having the time of his life at junior soccer practice.

It wasn't that she doubted Ashley's competence, but this was the first time she had left Jamie since he'd been given the all-clear by the doctors.

Up to this point, any trip away from home had deliberately *not* included an overnight stay, or if it had, she had taken Jamie with her. This was a big step for her, though less so, it seemed, for Jamie, who had been too busy playing with a new computer game to do more than give her a casual wave before he got back to his screen.

On one level she knew that he was fine, he was safe, and she knew her fear had no basis in logic but, as she had already discovered, it wasn't always about logic. When you had lived with fear this long it was something that was hard to let go of. For so long she had been afraid of losing her precious son and— She took a deep breath and deliberately dampened the panic she could feel rising. No, she told herself, repeating the phrase like a mantra, she was *not* going to lose him, because he was healthy now.

Her son was a survivor, one of the lucky ones, and he had made a complete recovery. Despite the fact he was noticeably smaller and more delicate-looking than his contemporaries, Jamie was, so the medics told her, as fit and robust as any other four-year-old and would soon catch up developmentally.

The assistant manager cleared his throat and lowered his tablet. 'We do have an alternative room although it is not as—'

'That's tremendous, thank you so much. I'll take it.'

Reaching for her sunglasses, she slid them on her small straight nose, hiding behind the tinted glass as she dredged deep to produce a faint smile.

'Right then, if you can give me a few moments I will make the necessary arrangements. The room is on the second floor—will that do?'

'That's fine. It's just the balcony up here that bothers me.' She stopped, well aware that the balcony she spoke of was not actually visible from where they stood.

'I understand totally.'

Luckily for her he didn't.

'I will be back momentarily.' He held out a straight-backed chair situated by a small table and after a pause she took it.

'Can I get you anything?'

She made an inarticulate sound in her throat and vaguely registered the sound of the door closing, the images floating in her head exerting a tug she couldn't resist.

She was standing on the balcony that she knew existed behind the heavy curtains in the bedroom. It was night, as dark outside as a city ever got, and she was staring down at the shining lights, the glistening moisture on the rain-soaked pavements, when she felt the quivering downy hair rise on her skin a second before the back of her neck started to tingle—she was no longer alone.

Her breath left her lungs as his big strong hands came to rest on her shoulders. As if connected by an invisible thread to his body, she leaned back against his chest, drawn to the hard warmth of his maleness, breathing in the clean unique fragrance of him. For a few moments they stayed that way, her heart beating heavy and slow in anticipation for a long while before he twisted her around to face him, and, like a parched flower turning to the sun, her face had tilted as she had strained upwards to meet his cool, firm lips with her own.

The languid heat that had spread through her body like a flash fire had made her bones dissolve and she would have slid to the floor had a muscular arm not banded her narrow ribcage before he'd picked her up and...!

Behind the smoky lenses of her sunglasses her pupils dilated as she swallowed hard, pushing the memory kicking and screaming back into its box. She glanced at the bedroom door again and felt her insides tighten.

With a cry she shot to her feet, opened the suite door a crack and positioned herself within reaching distance of the door handle for a quick escape should she need it, before pressing her rigid shoulder blades against the wall and closing her eyes...

What were the odds of finding herself in the exact same suite?

Fighting to keep her thoughts in the here and now, which, no matter how uncomfortable, was infinitely preferable to obsessing about the past, she took another deep mind-clearing breath.

She was winning and then she just *had to* sabotage her own progress and peek through the open bedroom door and see that bed. With no warning the past collided painfully with the present again with a concussive impact.

'No!' Teeth clenched, she ran across the room and closed the door with a decisive click before leaning her back against it, even though she knew a couple of inches of wood was no defence against the memories that had been playing in a loop ever since she'd got out of the taxi and found herself standing in the exact spot where it had all begun more than five years earlier.

Suddenly, she was feeling the rain from that day over five years ago beating down from a leaden sky, plastering her water-darkened hair to her head, much longer then than the shoulder-blade length she favoured now.

The soaked strands kept getting in her eyes, though with her head down against the driving force of the cloudburst all she could see were people's feet and the standing water on the pavement increasing in depth with each passing moment.

It had taken seconds for the thin linen jacket

she was wearing to become totally saturated, her bare legs below the denim skirt she was wearing were slick with rain and her feet in wedge sandals squelched as she avoided another lethal umbrella that was being wielded like a shield. Any trace of make-up was a mere memory, and she gave up brushing away the droplets trembling on the ends of her long curling eyelashes before falling into her eyes.

It had seemed like such a good idea when she'd been sitting waiting for Rupert to come out of his weekly appointment with his oncologist, less so now. But when the page of the glossy magazine she had picked up had opened on an advert for the opening of the new London branch of the famous Parisian chocolatier that Rupert, with his sweet tooth, adored, it had seemed like something nice to do for the man to whom she owed so much.

Rupert, the man who legally at least she was married to, had called their arrangement *symbiotic* when he had offered her an escape route from the seemingly endless nightmare she had fallen into after her father's death, but to her it often seemed more like a one-sided deal.

She wasn't even sure that this mysterious

debt Rupert had claimed he owed her father existed, though the men's friendship certainly had. Her father had been a man with a lot of friends; he'd been funny, articulate, generous to a fault and he'd thrown legendary parties—of course he'd had friends. Only for the most part, they'd turned out to be the variety that had disappeared when it had become public knowledge after his death that, despite his lifestyle, there had been no money left, just debts.

His death was the only thing that had kept the bailiffs temporarily away from the door of the lovely home she was living in that was mortgaged up to the hilt. The staff had not been paid for two months, though selling her jewellery had dealt with that issue, and everything else would have to be sold too: the fleet of cars in the garage; her father's share in the racehorse that never won anything but cost a bomb in trainers, stables and veterinary bills.

She'd been poor before, that was not a problem for Marisa, but what had been a nightmare was the money that the lawyers said her father owed, and not all the debts, she'd soon learnt, were owed to legitimate sources. Some, the ones whose sinister representatives Marisa had come home from the funeral to find sitting uninvited in her living room, were not inclined to stand in line to be paid a fraction of what they were owed.

They'd wanted their money right then, all of it, and the dark consequences they'd hinted at should she not come up with the goods had been chilling enough, though not as much as the stomach-curdling suggestion that she could reduce the debt by being *nice* to important friends of their clients.

She had still been shaking with reaction to the crude suggestion when Rupert had arrived. He'd sat her down, poured her a stiff brandy and had teased the story out of her. It was then that he'd shared his own shocking news, explaining not just his medical diagnosis, but that his disease was terminal. He considered it a private matter, he didn't want her sympathy, and wasn't afraid to die—he was ready.

What he didn't want, he'd told her, was to die alone, and he'd been alone ever since the death of the love of his life, a man whose funeral Rupert hadn't even been able to attend because his long-time lover had had a wife and family who didn't know, or didn't want to know, that he had been gay.

Marriage to Marisa, he'd said, would make everything so much easier legally after he died—*she'd* actually be helping *him*. And, for some reason he'd refused to disclose, he'd owed it to her father to ensure she was safe. Marisa, ignoring the voice of conscience in the back of her mind, had let herself believe him. Grief-stricken, desperate and so very alone, she'd agreed.

They had married in a civil ceremony a week later. There had been no honeymoon but they'd shared a bottle of champagne, and that had been the first time Rupert had told her upfront, to her acute embarrassment, that it would be fine with him if she wanted a life outside their marriage. If she had friends, *male* friends, he'd added, in case she hadn't got his drift.

She had got it, but, as she had informed him there and then, that wouldn't be an issue for her and she had meant it. She had never been a particularly *physical* person and she had always avoided intimacy of that nature. What she'd been looking for in a relationship was what she had always craved: safety and stability.

School friends had always envied Marisa her adventurous lifestyle, not knowing about the unpaid bills that her father had cheerfully binned whenever the drawer he'd shoved them into had got full, never dreaming that their friend, who got to mingle with famous people and order her dinner from room service in five-star hotels, instead longed for the security of their boring lives.

Ironically she now had the dreamt-of security, although this had never been the way she had visualised it coming about, and up to a point it had worked. But to her, at least, it was becoming more obvious with each passing day that there was nothing *equal* about her and Rupert's deal, and there was a certain irony in the fact that her attempt to assuage her guilt in a small way had set in motion a sequence of events that would lead to her act of betrayal. And no matter that Rupert had virtually given his blessing to her taking lovers, for Marisa, what she had done remained a betrayal.

Waiting until Rupert was taking his afternoon nap she had set off to purchase his surprise treat, taking the shortcut through the park because it was such a lovely afternoon—or at least it had been, until the heavens opened and the rain came pelting down!

She was just wondering whether there was any point getting a taxi when she sidestepped a puddle and walked full pelt into a person— or it could have been a steel wall; the amount of *give* was about the same—the impact driving the air from her lungs in a sharp gasp as she bounced off him, very nearly losing her balance.

Grappling with the distracting sensation of hardness and warmth left by the moment of contact while trying to keep her balance, she was saved the embarrassment and pain of landing on her bottom in a puddle by a pair of large hands that shot out, spanning her waist and quite literally putting her back on her feet.

'I'm so, so sorry…' She began tilting her chin to look up…a long way, as it turned out, but as she finally made it to the face of the man who still had his hands on her waist she promptly forgot what she was going to say, the clutching sensation in the pit of her stomach giving way to a shallow gasp of shock.

She now knew why it had felt as though she were walking into a wall. Everything about the stranger was hard. He was lean, broad-shouldered and several inches over six feet; the long drovers raincoat he wore open over a suit and tie did not disguise the muscular athleticism of his body.

If the physical impact had snatched her breath away, the impact as her gaze collided with the dark heavy-lidded eyes of the stranger made her heart almost stop beating, the raw masculinity he projected like nothing she had ever encountered before in her twenty-one years. Strange, scary sensations were zigzagging through her body, as though her nervous system had just received a million-volt hit.

It was the weirdest sensation. The noise of other people, the busy traffic, the storm raging overhead were all still there but they receded into the background. Instead, her world had contracted into the space, the air molecules between her and this man... There was just this extraordinary man, and he really was the most beautiful thing she had ever seen in her life!

She knew she was staring at him but she couldn't stop. His strong-jawed oval face was all sculpted cheekbones, carved planes and intriguing angles, and the skin stretched over bones of perfect striking symmetry was a deep vibrant bronzed gold. Looking at his firm, sensually moulded mouth sent her core temperature up several painful degrees—it was a sinful miracle.

The thick brows above his eyes lifted and she couldn't help noticing that they were as black as the curling lashes that framed his deep-set dark, quizzical eyes.

'Are you all right?'

He had an *almost* accent—it was there somewhere in the perfect diction and the deep, smooth drawl. There was a smile and something else in his eyes that was as lushly velvet as his voice.

It was the something else that intensified the violent quivering in the pit of her stomach.

She lifted a hand to push the hair from her cheek, the rain-soaked strands tangling in her slim fingers while beneath the film of moisture her face felt hot.

'Fine, fine... I'm fine.' And surprisingly she was, for someone who had quite clearly lost her mind and couldn't stop shaking.

She just hoped the internal tremors did not show on the outside, but she realised that on the plus side she would no longer need to pretend to have a clue what people were talking about when they mentioned lust at first sight.

On the minus side, she knew in a distant corner of her mind that she was making a total fool of herself because she didn't have the skill or the experience to hide what she was feeling.

His incredible cynical eyes said he knew *exactly* what was happening between them.

'You're wet,' he said, dragging a hand across his own hair, removing the excess moisture from the jet-black strands, then he reversed the gesture, causing his hair to stand up in sexy damp spikes. As he stood there just staring at her, Marisa had the oddest feeling he could see the thoughts swirling in her head, so maybe that was why he suddenly said abruptly, 'Would you like to come inside?'

'Inside...?' she echoed stupidly.

Without taking his eyes from her face, he gestured with a tip of his head towards the entrance of the Madrigal Hotel.

She paused long enough so that he had to know she'd considered it before she began to babble, hating the breathy sound of her own panicked voice as she took refuge in good manners.

'No, no, I'm fine. I'm sorry I got you wet and thank you for...' She stopped short, figuring she had already made herself look as ridiculous as it was humanly possible to. She shook her head but didn't move, her soggy feet feeling as glued to the ground as her eyes were to the face of this tall, imposing stranger.

He arched a dark brow. 'Well, if you change your mind I'm here all week.'

His offer, if that was what it was, broke her free of the paralysis that had gripped her, and with another shake of her head, this time with her eyes safely on the pavement in front of her, she turned around and in seconds was lost amongst the body of people surging along the wet pavement. Her heart was pounding so loudly it felt like a sonar locator as she rushed on, welcoming the cooling caress of the rain as it hit her hot face.

After the initial surge of relief that she'd escaped—from exactly what was not a question she wanted to explore—she found herself wondering what would have happened if she had accepted the stranger's invitation.

Really, Marisa, you're not that naïve, are you? mocked the voice in her head as she squelched along, the rain numbing the heat of embarrassment in her cheeks. Or was that *excitement*?

That would have been the end of it, and *should* have been the end of it had fate and her school friend Cressy's domestic emergency not intervened.

'It would be good,' Cressy had said when they'd bumped into one another the previous week, 'to catch up.'

It was the sort of vague, socially polite thing that people said without actually meaning it and Marisa had responded in the same vein, never for a second expecting to be asked to follow through.

But Cressy had invited her out for a meal, and in the end it had been Rupert, so cheered at the prospect of her getting out, who had made her agree.

That evening she left him with his chocolates and a video of his favourite film and went out, and it was actually quite nice to dress up and get out of her comfortable clothes for once.

That was the funny thing about clothes—especially when you added some bold red lipstick—and she left the house looking everything she knew she wasn't: sexy and confident.

Cressy, who was still struggling, she said, with her post-baby body, pronounced herself envious, but when Marisa watched her face as she scrolled proudly through the photos of her husband and baby twin boys on her phone Marisa knew her old friend was lying. Cressy wouldn't swap what she had for a size-eight figure and a few glamorous outfits!

They had not even selected their food when Cressy received the phone call from home.

'Yes, give him one spoonful if his temperature is up. It's in the bathroom cabinet in the boys' room, top shelf. Yes, I know you'll be fine and I will have fun... Love you...' Cressy slid the phone back in her clutch bag but she gave Marisa a rueful look and sighed. 'Sorry, Marisa, but...'

'Rain check. Don't worry, I get it. You go home...make sure your boys are all right.'

Cressy's relief was obvious.

Marisa finished her own cocktail and the one Cressy had not touched, and it was still only nine p.m. She was left all dressed up with nowhere to go but home again, where Rupert, who always retired early, would already be in bed, helped by the live-in nurse who had been with them for a few weeks now. Marisa decided to walk back as it was a lovely evening, and somehow she found herself standing outside the Madrigal, which was *almost* on her way home.

The stranger wouldn't be there, she reasoned, shivering as she thought of him. It was still so early…why not go in for a nightcap? She'd always wanted to see what the Madrigal was like inside and she was certainly dressed for it.

A combination of self-delusion and the cocktails that were not as innocuous as they'd looked got her through the doors and into the expensive-smelling wood-panelled foyer when the reality of what she was doing hit her, shame and mind-clearing horror following close behind.

She turned and would have headed back

through the door had a voice not suddenly nailed her feet to the Aubusson carpet.

'Would you like a drink?'

Shocked recognition and stomach-tightening excitement grabbed her as, her breath coming faster, she spun back slowly on her heels.

With her heart trying to batter its way through her ribcage, her eyes travelled in an upward sweep over the long, lean length of his body, clad this evening in a beautifully cut dark grey suit, underneath which was a pale blue shirt open at the neck to reveal the tanned brown skin of his throat, and fine enough to suggest the musculature of his chest and torso. The expensive tailoring didn't do anything to lessen the aura of raw, head-spinning masculinity he projected.

'No, I didn't come here for—' She blinked and stopped. What had she come here for?

Exactly what he thinks you did, the voice in her head responded.

He took a step forward and held out his hand. 'I'm Roman Bardales.'

After the faintest hesitation she reached out, a shock of electricity of a lethal voltage running through her body as his warm brown fingers closed around her hand and didn't move, and she saw his polished brown eyes widen as though he too had felt the same stinging shock.

'Marisa Rayner.' She pulled her hand away.

'I'm glad you came.'

'I... I didn't...' One darkly delineated brow lifted to a sardonic angle and she rushed on. 'Well, I am here.'

'So I see.' The comprehensive sweep of his brown eyes as they slid over her body made her shiver. 'And now?'

'Now?' She had to force the word past the ache in her dry throat.

'Are you coming up?' The slight jerk of his head was directed at the lift behind him.

He didn't say for a coffee, or a nightcap, because they both knew that wasn't why she was there.

'I... I don't do things like this.'

'OK,' he said slowly in acknowledgment, and then he did nothing else to influence her decision besides standing there looking gorgeous enough to melt her bones.

Marisa had known deep down that she was just going through the motions pretending to delay. The decision had already been made as soon as she had made her way to the hotel this evening. Her struggle now was for appearances—her own, not his.

His impressive shoulders lifted in the faintest of shrugs. 'We could go for a walk instead?'

She shook her head. 'No, I'll…' She expelled a deep breath and started to move towards the lifts.

CHAPTER TWO

THE YOUNGEST ADDITION to the Bardales company was anxious to make a good impression, having checked and double-checked everything on board the private jet was as it should be. Instead of joining the other staff, who were chatting and drinking coffee while they waited for their passenger to arrive, Alex made his way down the steps looking for the chief steward to ask if there was anything else he could do.

He was a shiny foot off the tarmac of the private landing strip when he spotted the man he was looking for in conversation with the plane's pilot. Probably not the best idea to disturb them, he decided. Besides, there was such a thing as being *too* keen.

Alex was about to turn and retrace his steps when he spotted the cloud of dust in the distance on the road that snaked its way across the red earth with the mountains as a stunning backdrop.

He paused, watching the cloud of dust getting nearer, feeling a pang of envy as the sleek outline of the designer car emerged, barely slowing its breakneck speed as it passed through the tall security gates that magically opened as it approached.

The car drew to a halt on the tarmac and a tall, dark-haired figure emerged. He slammed the door hard enough to take it off its hinges and removed a pair of dark shades, tucking them into a pocket before sweeping the area with eyes that, even at this distance, appeared arctic cold to the new recruit. Alex took an involuntary step backwards, experiencing a stab of relief when a member of the security team, a fellow newcomer, moved forward to intercept the stranger, albeit without a lot of enthusiasm, and who could blame him? The broad-shouldered figure was emanating an aura of danger that enveloped his frame as visibly as the dust had enveloped his supercar.

Alex looked on curiously as the security guard moved back again…everyone present on the landing strip was stepping back to allow the unimpeded progress of the tall man, who looked capable of demolishing anything that got in his way.

Initially confused, Alex began to make more sense of the scene as the figure got close enough for him to recognise the carved contours of his face—some sense at least, but now the confusion remained for another reason.

Did his employer lead a double life?

True, Alex had never met the man in person, but he'd seen him in a photo when he'd pored over the company website before his interview, until he'd felt he knew everything about the Bardales brand that stood, so the logo proclaimed, for ethical quality.

In the photos the head of the company had looked sharply tailored and pristine; today he was wearing faded jeans that possessed more than a few frayed holes that had certainly not been placed there by any designer, and a dark tee shirt that clung to the well-developed contours of his powerful chest and bagged around his washboard-flat belly, giving a glimpse of the muscle ridges there, his dusty boots kicking up little flurries of earth as he walked.

In every photo Alex had ever seen, his

employer's black hair had been fashionably cropped, but the man approaching now wore it long enough to curl on his neck with enough length on top to cause it to cover his strongly delineated dark brows. At regular intervals he swept it back with an impatient long-fingered brown hand.

The aquiline features looked to have the same carved symmetry of the internet version, though it was hard to tell as the previously clean-shaven lines were heavily dusted with facial hair that stopped just short of being a beard and gave its owner a look that could only be called menacing.

Looks, his mother always said, could be deceptive. Alex really hoped so because this man's appearance alone would have made any person with an ounce of common sense cross the street to avoid him, and he considered himself very sensible.

'Roman…!'

Alex registered the genuine warmth in the pilot's voice as the older man stepped briskly forward, skirting the plane and moving towards the new arrival, and comprehension finally dawned.

So this man was actually Rio Bardales's *brother*, the identical twin who, the carefully worded website blurb had explained, did not at this point take an active part in company operations. It had gone on to list the several innovations and successful financial ventures that this currently absent Bardales twin *had* been responsible for, before briefly mentioning his new career as a bestselling author.

Well, it wasn't exactly a secret. Alex had still been at school when Roman Bardales had been outed as the author of the bestselling thriller series that had taken the popular literature world by storm. Since then Hollywood had expanded the audience for the exploits of the enigmatic flawed hero of his books—Danilo, a man of few words with a taste for fast cars, extreme sports and beautiful brainy women, though the only permanent fixture in his life was his Czech wolf-dog, who was the canine version of his enigmatic lone-wolf master.

The publicity machine claimed Roman Bardales cared deeply about realism and that he never had his hero perform a feat he hadn't already mastered himself. Shots of him clinging, not a rope in sight, to the sheer rock face of

a mountain with a dizzying drop below suggested this might not be all hype.

Alex had not read any of the books but he
was a massive fan of the films—his friends
were going to be so jealous when he told them.
Maybe he would get to shake his hand? Or
even—

'No, don't ask for his autograph.'

The youngster spun around. 'I wasn't—' he
began, his voice fading and his blush bloom-
ing as the senior steward gave him a knowing
look and then suggested, not unkindly, that he
might like to do some work.

It took a few moments for the sound of the familiar voice to penetrate the zone Roman had
occupied for the entirety of his drive. It was
a technique he used when he climbed. You
didn't think ahead, you just lived in the moment and focused on the next move, because
if your mind wandered, if you allowed yourself to be distracted, the consequences could
be life-threatening or, at the very least, life
altering.

Today the danger was not an unforgiving
two-hundred-foot drop below his dangling

feet, and it was not a rock face he was clinging to by his fingernails, it was his rage. The moment he started thinking more than one move ahead the red mist threatened to consume him all over again and he had to stop thinking again... His eyes slid to his clenched right fist and the broken skin on his knuckles.

He flexed his hand, and rubbed it against his thigh. He and his twin had had any number of arguments before, some more heated than others. It was inevitable when two strong-minded individuals were involved—the clash of the alphas, their mother called it.

The thought of their remaining parent lifted one corner of his mouth, softening his expression for a second or two before it flattened again. This time, his and Rio's argument had been different; it had been...*visceral*.

It wasn't just the punch he had landed on his brother, it was the fact he had not wanted to stop hitting him, but Rio, *damn him*, wouldn't defend himself and he... Roman took a deep breath and let it out slowly, his thoughts drifting back to their recent encounter, a memory that would take a lot more than time to heal.

When his twin had begged him to hear him

out, Roman had acquiesced, sprawling in one of the chairs, trying to hide his smile as he'd resisted the temptation to tease his twin a little. At that point he'd still been assuming his brother's confession had something to do with the cosy domestic scenario he had walked in on. It seemed Rio had a kid he'd not known about…and the kid's mother appeared to be in his dedicated bachelor brother's life too. Roman could see why that story might necessitate the deep breath his brother took before he'd started to speak.

He had allowed his brother to get to the end of his story. As it turned out, it wasn't a story about Rio's own domestic arrangements, but there was a secret child involved. Only it wasn't Rio's daughter, it was *Roman's* son.

Roman's smile was long gone when he'd got to his feet, and it had been replaced by a ferocious scowl as he'd moved across the room until he'd stood toe to toe, shoulder to shoulder, with his identical twin.

'Marisa…' *His* Marisa, except of course she wasn't his, she was someone else's Marisa and she always had been, even while she'd been in his bed, while she was making him feel…

Roman shook his head fiercely. It had all been a lie; even his own feelings, feelings that had felt real at the time, had been only an illusion, but the child was definitely real. 'She came to *you*?'

'It wasn't easy for her.'

The sympathy in his brother's eyes had only added insult to injury, and the feral sound that had escaped his compressed white-edged lips had risen up from some deep place inside his belly as he'd stood there clenching every muscle and sinew.

'But she was desperate. There was nowhere else for her to go.'

'How about me? If she'd needed a bone-marrow donor for her son, preferably a *"related"* compatible donor—' his lips curled as he drew mocking quotation marks in the air before his voice dropped to a base boom of fury '—then why not come to me if I'm the child's father?'

His stabbing finger stopped just short of his brother's chest, but Rio hadn't flinched an inch, he had just stood there looking as guilty as hell. *A bit late for that, brother!*

'Because you—' Rio had visibly bitten down on what he'd been about to say and finished flatly. 'We've got the same DNA. The child urgently needed a bone-marrow transplant from a…yes…preferably related donor. Should I have refused her request?'

'You *should* have told me…and because *what*? What were you going to say about why she hadn't come to me instead of you?'

'Because,' his brother had finally flung at him, 'you were all over the tabloids with that blonde flashing her ample cleavage in your face while coyly saying in a totally unconvincing way that your relationship was strictly professional. I had no reason to disbelieve the rumours that you were about to get engaged— and you certainly didn't deny it.'

'It *was* purely professional,' Roman had gritted back, dismissing the irrelevance with a wave of his hand. 'Petra was an agent for the film distribution company liaising with the publisher.' And a great loss to the acting profession.

The first time she had displayed her stage skills, Roman hadn't seen the cameras, so he hadn't had a clue what was going on when she had whipped off her glasses, unfastened several buttons of her blouse and plastered herself against him, her myopic blue eyes sending him a warning dagger look as she'd muttered an instruction to *'play along'*, snuggling up to him before displaying a very realistic shock when a series of camera flashes had exploded in their faces.

She had earnestly backed up his stony declarations of 'No comment' with a fluttering display of denials guaranteed to look suspect.

Roman didn't like this reminder of poor judgement on his part. Initially Petra's machinations had amused him and it hadn't seemed important then, so he had allowed the situation to go on longer than he should have. By the end, though, Petra had been in danger of forgetting she was acting—or that might have been an act too, for all he knew.

'Professional?'

He'd scowled at his brother's scepticism. 'A trade-off, then. The film company execs were throwing fits because I had refused to participate in a promotional tour of the latest movie and I don't give interviews, so they figured that, because everyone loves the idea of a romance, the occasional photo op with Petra would keep me and, more importantly, the film, on the front pages, without me having to say a word. I really don't see what that has to do with anything.'

'Then you really are stupid as well as forgetful.'

'So because I am stupid *you* decided that you would ride to the rescue and save *my* child while taking it upon yourself to conceal the fact I even had a child from me—and now you thought you'd ease your conscience by confessing all. Tell me, Rio, whose idea was it not to tell me in the first place? Yours or Marisa's? Did you offer her a shoulder to cry on? Yes, I can just see it now...' And he had, so vividly, been able to see Marisa's blonde head on his brother's shoulder, her soft body pressed against Rio's hard one... The taunting images had flashed in front of his eyes, and he'd furiously shrugged off Rio's placatory hand on his shoulder.

'I don't expect you to forgive me, Roman, but I truly meant it for the best—'

Playing the scene over and over again in his head, Roman was sure that Rio had seen the fist coming but he'd made no attempt to avoid it, he'd just stood there waiting for the punch to land.

Roman had left his brother lying on the floor, rubbing his jaw and staunching the nose bleed he'd acquired from hitting the coffee table on his way down, and had walked away, or at least had driven away at high speed. It had been thirty minutes later that he had realised he didn't have a clue where he was driving to, as for once his legendary sense of direction had deserted him.

As he'd drawn over to the side of the empty road he'd remembered his twin's penultimate words... *'The jet will be waiting for you when you need it.'*

Roman had rejected the offer out of hand. 'You think I'm going to chase after her?'

'I thought you might like to see your son. If I were you, I would. They are in England.'

'You're not me, though, are you? And you can keep your nose the hell out of my business! I'm finished with you!'

Now the red mist had cleared, the fact there was a jet ready and willing to take him where he needed to go was not so inconvenient.

'Santiago.' Drawing his attention back to the here and now, Roman tipped his head in acknowledgment to the man who had been responsible for both him and his twin getting their pilot's licences, as the older man walked over, his hand extended.

The handshake morphed into a manly clap on the shoulder before the pilot stepped away, searching his face.

Something in his calm steady gaze lowered Roman's tension a couple of notches. 'It's been a long time, Santiago.'

'Two years, but who's counting? Oh, and thanks for the tip—still keeping your hand in, then?'

Roman looked blank for a moment, then a grin flashed momentarily, lightening the sombre set of his carved features. 'You invested in Raoul's start-up, then, like I recommended?'

The older man nodded. 'I'd still be kicking myself if I hadn't. Your friend wouldn't have any problem raising money these days, would he? They say the simplest ideas are the best, and I'm glad they're right. I have a nice pension fund for when I'm too old to fly these things any more.' He glanced towards the fuelled and waiting plane then turned his attention back to the man who co-owned it. 'You really can't *help* making money, can you?'

A cloud passed across Roman's face, cancelling out the half-smile and darkening his eyes. 'I get it from my father.' Unfortunately the ability to make money was not the only thing he had inherited from his father. It seemed he'd also acquired the rage and the jealousy that had dogged his parents' marriage.

'I don't remember him having your way with words, though. I read your last book.' Santiago's bushy brows lifted as his glance slid up from Roman's dusty boots to his windswept head, taking in everything in between. 'You been doing a photoshoot for your next cover? Channelling the inner lean and mean?'

Roman's uncomfortable grimace made Santiago's grin deepen, though underneath the laconic amusement he was relieved to see another slight lessening in the taut-tripwire level of tension that coiled the younger man's body tighter than an overwound steel spring on the point of snapping.

* * *

'I hear that you never write any hero stunt you haven't done yourself?'

'Don't believe everything you read. How is Meg?' Roman felt ashamed that his own self-centred concerns meant it had taken this long for him to ask.

'She's still in remission, and we're both enjoying it. You should try it.'

'What?' Roman said as he walked alongside the other man towards the plane.

'Marriage.'

'I'm not the marrying kind.'

But then again, you weren't the fathering kind, were you? And just look what happened.

'Neither was I until I met Meg.'

'The Megs of this world are rare.' The Marisas were rare too, but in a very different way.

The Marisas of this world lied their way into a man's head, made him think that she was as necessary as oxygen to him, and then went back to another man. Her *husband*. He had spent his life building up walls and she had knocked them down with one glance of those golden glowing, *hungry* eyes.

He let out another breath when the emotional

shields he had constructed withstood the memory, as well as the image of a face of cut-glass delicate beauty. His nostrils flared; he'd been played and it had hit him where it hurt most—in his pride—but he had moved on.

It had taken some time for him to appreciate the fact that she had actually done him a favour in refusing to leave her husband; his *collision* with Marisa had been the spur he'd needed to shake him out of the rut he'd been in and into an entirely new life. He'd cut ties he'd no longer needed, been liberated from responsibilities he'd no longer wanted. He relied on no one but himself and no one relied on him; wasn't that the very definition of freedom…?

The unacknowledged question mark that accompanied the thought twitched his dark brows into a frown that deepened as his thoughts took the next logical leap forward. Now he had a son, and that was a responsibility he couldn't walk away from.

It was a responsibility he was running towards.

Maybe someone should warn the kid, mocked the sardonic voice in his head.

He tensed, unwilling even to acknowledge

the deep-seated fear in his belly; it was an old fear that he'd always lived with. It was this fear and not a whim that had influenced his decision not to become a father. It was the responsible thing to do when you realised there was too much of your own father in you. Roman had intended to break the cycle because he didn't want his legacy to be an emotionally damaged child. *Dios*, this wasn't meant to be happening—there shouldn't *be* a child.

He'd taken precautions, but everyone except an idiot knew the only foolproof form of contraception was total abstinence, and that option had been off the table from the moment he'd seen her standing in the lobby balanced on crazy heels that made her incredible legs look endless and wearing a mere sliver of silk that had clung to her sleek curves like a lover's caress.

'You joining me?' Santiago nodded towards the cockpit.

Roman moved his head as if to dislodge the circling mesh of thoughts. 'Not this time,' he replied.

There were some familiar staff members on the flight and others less so, but he felt too drained to make the effort to even acknowledge the nods of recognition.

Fighting impatience, he took a seat and belted up. The effort of maintaining even an illusion of normality was beyond him at that moment, and he found it hard to imagine there would be any moments of normality in his life ever again.

He had a child!

When would it seem real to him? Hands clenched, knuckles bone white, he pressed his head into the backrest and allowed his eyes to close, the sweep of his dark lashes casting an extra shadow that highlighted the jutting carved contours of his high cheekbones. Inside his head the rapid thoughts and questions, the *anger*, carried on swirling, and, yes, even though he had pushed it right to the back of his mind, there was still the fear lurking, fear that he would do to his child what his father had done to him.

You're so like your father!

How old had he been the first time he had heard those words? Far too young—and he'd heard them far too many times since.

High too was the number of times he had

watched his father bully, berate and belittle his mother, or seen the signs of an imminent meltdown as his father's face had become suffused with anger and his eyes had gone cold before he'd flown into a rage.

Roman had always used the same silent mantra on these occasions—*I am not like him. I won't be that man.*

The childish determination had morphed into an adult resolution that had made him the man he was today, the man who was aware of the need to keep his emotions under control, to never want anything or anyone so much that it became a dangerous obsession.

If that made him someone who was considered to be remote and emotionless he could live with that, and being called heartless by ex-lovers was not a high price to pay in his eyes.

No female had ever accessed the wild, dark inner depths of him until Marisa had walked into his life, and, to his horror, all the dormant suppressed emotions he'd always sensed were there had roared into life, his response to her primal and uncontrolled.

His jaw clenched as he tried to silence the memories. What he needed was…what?

He needed to *do* something—inactivity was not something he had ever mastered, and his usual ability to sleep anywhere any time had deserted him. There was too much time for thinking, for the frustration curdling in his gut to expand until he felt as if he'd explode!

Deaf to the polite question of the attendant standing at his elbow, he pressed his hands on the armrests and vaulted to his feet in one smooth motion, causing the attendant to take an involuntary step back.

He dragged his hair back from his forehead. The combined effects of the shock revelation and lack of sleep were beginning to kick in hard, but control was his bedrock, his strength, and although he had to dig deep he was able to stretch his mouth into something approaching a smile.

'No...no, thank you,' he said with a shake of his head. 'I'm just going to—' Gesturing in the direction of the adjoining compartment, he swiftly headed for the privacy of the bedroom suite.

Any personal items his twin might have left in there had been stowed away except for a snapshot of him and his brother tucked into the frame of the full-length mirror. He strode across, focusing on the snapshot rather than his own reflection, and two identical faces stared back at him. He felt something shift in his chest but before he could put a name to the emotion, he looked away quickly, directing his stare at his mirrored reflection.

Turning away again to avoid the accusation in the bleak dark eyes staring back at him, he retrieved his phone from the pocket where he had shoved it after he'd glanced at the replies to the stream of texts he'd sent once he'd rung ahead to commandeer the jet.

Scan reading was a useful skill but he wanted to be sure he had not missed any detail, though it was the missing details that were harder to deal with, or at least one in particular. It seemed unlikely that there was not a single photo of his son, James Alexander, in the public domain, but the investigative firm he was dealing with had always been efficient in the past.

He scrolled through the email and it didn't take long—it was short and to the point. The more in-depth report would land in his inbox in the next twenty-four hours as he'd been promised. There were a few extras, like Marisa's date of birth and her marital status, which he already knew... His thumb paused over the screen, his heart pounding as he discovered a detail he had not picked up first time around. Marisa Rayner was now a widow.

His mouth twisted into a cynical smile. At least his son would not be calling another man Father; other than that the detail was not relevant to him.

His glance returned to the stand-out detail that had drawn a smile of the blackest kind from him. The irony of it was darker than night. Marisa was to be found, with or without his son—that piece of information was apparently not available—in the five-star luxury of the Madrigal Hotel—the very same place where his son had been conceived.

His son!

He made a supreme effort and closed the lid on his rage. He would save it until he could vent it on the appropriate person. He made himself read the limited information once more, slowly and carefully.

No, he had it all memorised now; Marisa

was a guest speaker at a fundraising international event being held at the Madrigal.

It didn't say if she was combining business with pleasure.

Not that he gave a damn who she slept with, he told himself. Marisa was not his business, but his son was.

It was perfectly legitimate for him to feel anger at the prospect of her introducing another man he had not vetted into his child's life, but she could take who she liked to her bed.

He could not imagine a woman with her sexual appetites being alone for long. Maybe she was a creature of habit and the Madrigal was her hunting ground.

It was a place to which he had never intended to return, as it was the scene of his complete humiliation. For months afterwards, what had happened had played on an unceasing loop in his head.

He remembered every word of his proposal, the ones he had got out anyway. Before he had got halfway through his prepared speech or even opened the box containing the ring he'd so carefully picked out, she'd begged him to stop.

'Roman, please don't say anything more. I came here today to tell you I can't go on seeing you.'

'You love me.' He could still hear the certainty in his voice, his utter unshakeable conviction.

The memory of Marisa's soft husky voice cracking as she had begged him not to say that still had the power to fill him with gut-tightening self-disgust.

'Please, Roman, don't do this. I don't... I can't...you don't understand. I can't marry you because I already have a husband.'

'That can't be true!'

Initially he had thought her confession was an invention. The discovery after the first night they'd spent together that she was a virgin had shaken him. Part of him had been angry that she had given him this gift with no warning, but another part of him had been totally aroused that he had been her first lover.

'It is a marriage of...of convenience. There is no... We are not...' Crazy, considering what they had shared, she'd blushed before adding with husky self-consciousness '…intimate.'

'Then what the hell are you?'

'We are just friends,' she'd said softly. 'And I respect him more than any other person I know. I owe him so much and I won't leave him…'

Roman had done a quick translation.

'You mean you married him for his money! Well, sweetheart, you should have waited, because if that is what attracts you to men, I've got a lot more.'

She'd flinched but then continued quietly, 'I've hurt you and I'm so very sorry… I shouldn't have done any of this. It's all my fault and I know I wish I could go back and undo it…'

Roman caught another glimpse of his face in the mirror, seeing something in the eyes that looked back at him that he hadn't seen in a long time. It belonged to the days, weeks and months when he had been chained to the memories of being with her. He had finally escaped those memories, although it had meant reinventing himself, and he would not be going back except to claim his son.

What are you going to do with him when you've got him, Roman, or doesn't it matter so long as she doesn't have him?

Tuning out the sardonic voice in his head, he lifted a hand to his jaw, grimacing as he dragged it down over the rough three-day growth.

The self-mocking grin that tugged up the corners of his mouth only served to increase the look of bad-boy smouldering menace. It was a look that would open more than a few doors, but it wasn't bedrooms Roman was interested in right now.

Beneath the thick mat of stubble the slight cleft in his square chin deepened as he imagined the reaction if he strode into the foyer of the hotel where Marisa was staying.

He narrowed his eyes and leaned in closer, touching his hair-roughened cheek and jaw again. The bottom line was, he looked like a hardened bastard with trouble written all over him, which was an effective look most of the time considering the sort of action-man hero with emotional issues that he wrote about.

It was less good when you wanted doors to open in the world in which Marisa moved, when you wanted people to look at you and see responsible *good* father material.

A good father... Would he be one? Was he capable of it?

His brother had a child and he did not seem to be afraid of fatherhood or of repeating the mistakes of their own father. Then again, his twin was not like their father at all. Not like Roman was.

Had there been a particular moment when he had realised that the things he hated about his father were actually there inside himself? Roman wasn't sure; he just knew that having a child was a risk he had not been willing to take.

Jaw clenched, he forcibly silenced the voices of doubt in his head that were alien to his nature. True, there were times when he could have reeled off a list of reasons why fatherhood was not a path he intended to take, but he knew that there was no point doing that now. Events had moved on and this was no a longer a choice that was his to make.

Hands flat on the tiled vanity surface, he surveyed his face carefully before reaching into a drawer and pulling out a cellophane-wrapped disposable razor. He needed to get into role because although in a perfect world appearances didn't count, in the real world they counted big-time.

After viewing his jaw from several angles he set to work. It took two razors but five minutes later he was moderately pleased with the close shave he had achieved. No way was he tackling his own hair; instead he would rely on the products he had no doubt his brother kept on board to tame it after he showered.

He walked through to the bedroom, opening one of the built-in wardrobes, not surprised when he discovered that conveniently his twin was still in the habit of keeping several changes of clothes on board.

He ignored the section devoted to casual wear, his long fingers flicking through the suits and shirts section before finally selecting a pale shirt still with the discreet designer tag attached, and a grey suit. He looked at the ties, lifting a hand to his neck with a grimace, imagining the confining tightness.

'Thank you, brother,' he said, a grim smile flashing as he threw the selection on the freshly made-up bed. The underwear in the drawers were all still in their wrappings and a moment later boxers and socks joined the suit, shirt and tie.

Compact but luxuriously appointed, the bathroom had a decent-sized shower that ran the entire width of one side of the compartment. Stripping off the clothes he'd been wearing for thirty-six hours straight, he let them fall in a crumpled heap on the floor.

He might not hit the gym the way he used to when he was working in an office, but his life for the past few years had involved enough physical activity to compensate for this lack.

Both brothers had always been competitive but, while Rio used to excel at team sports, Roman, not a natural team player, had gravitated in the direction of solo extreme sports where he was competing against himself, pushing his body to the limit, solo sailing, running, gymnastics and his lasting passion— rock climbing.

He'd discovered that solo climbing complemented his lifestyle as a writer; when his head was crowded with imaginary characters and convoluted plots he found climbing was the perfect way to switch off—and it had the added benefit of keeping him extremely fit too.

Fifteen minutes later he stood suited and booted before the mirror once again. It was amazing what a shave could achieve, he decided, and the slicked-back hair created a transformation so complete that it would have bewildered even the most sophisticated facial-recognition technology.

The suit, which was probably a perfect fit, felt tight and constricting across his shoulders though it hung perfectly. Roman ignored the feeling, glancing down at the only incongruity—his worn and dusty desert boots. But he wasn't willing to sacrifice comfort for appearances—his feet were a half-size bigger than his twin's.

When he eventually emerged from the plane onto the tarmac, nobody was looking at his boots. They were looking at him though. Many eyes followed the tall, dynamic figure with the perfect profile and the powerful aura, yet Roman remained oblivious to them all, his mind set only on his goal.

CHAPTER THREE

'OH, I'M SO SORRY, sir, but that suite is occupied,' the person behind the desk at the Madrigal told him.

Before Roman could react to the news that suite number one-four-four was not vacant, and in retrospect he could see there was something quite masochistic in requesting to revisit the scene of his humiliation, the assistant manager appeared at his elbow.

'Actually it is unexpectedly vacant.'

The suited figure produced a key card from his pocket like a magician and handed it to Roman.

A maid was emerging from the door to the suite as he approached. Roman smiled at her and watched her flush. He had already pulled the key card from his pocket when the thought came to him.

'Excuse me, miss…?' The girl swung back, her smile eager. 'I have a friend staying here, a Marisa Rayner…? I don't suppose you could tell me her room number.'

Her face fell. 'I'm sorry, sir, but that is not allowed.'

He sighed. 'I understand; it's just that it's her birthday and I wanted to surprise her…'

'Well, if you don't tell anyone it was me who told you…?'

'My lips are sealed,' he promised.

The screen went black and Marisa sighed and closed the laptop. She pressed her head back into the cushion, her neck feeling stiff with tension. The only question in her mind was did she take a shower before or after she read through her notes for tomorrow before she fell into bed?

She was definitely not going to think about that room somewhere above her head; she was already ashamed of her meltdown. It wasn't as if a room could hurt you, after all.

But memories could hurt and they did, even now. As did the sense of shame when she thought of those ten days when she had spent every moment she could in that room, in that bed, with Roman. It still felt like the actions of a stranger; she didn't know that person who had surrendered without a fight to the raw passion he had awoken inside her.

At least she felt a lot calmer now, especially after her reassuring report from Ashley and her chat with Jamie. Of course she was missing him but he didn't seem to be missing her at all, which was as it should be.

Her head lifted reluctantly in response to the knock on the door.

She huffed a breath and heaved herself tiredly to her feet. Stepping over her discarded shoes, she smoothed down her hair. If it was *another* fruit basket or chocolates she had no idea where they'd put it. Perhaps she ought to just tell the hotel staff she wasn't going to complain or give them any less than a five-star review because they had done nothing wrong.

She opened the door with a smile.

The rushing sensation of the floor coming up to meet her was so strong that she was surprised to find she was still standing upright.

Her skin bleached milk-pale as the electric surge reached her hands and feet and remained there in her tingling extremities. Her brain closed down for a split second, but when it kicked back in she stammered out a shocked but firm, 'No, this isn't actually happening.'

Roman would have taken more pleasure from her shocked reaction if he hadn't been experiencing a similar reaction himself.

He had been channelling pure rage and retribution as he'd waited for the hotel-room door to open, but it wasn't until it did that he realised it wasn't *pure* anything. What was superficially anger was actually far more complicated and multi-layered. When the door opened the combined force of his convoluted emotions hit him with such ferocity that it felled him, not literally, although he wouldn't have been at all surprised to discover he was lying at her feet.

He focused on the anger and not the empty ache inside him, though its existence made him mad as hell too, angry that the woman had made a fool of him, yet the sight of her had not just paralyzed him with lust, it had made him conscious of the emptiness inside him that he normally refused to acknowledge.

'Roman?'

His identity was not in question. What she ought to be asking instead was, *Why the hell are you standing outside my door?* A tiny choking sound left Marisa's lips as her eyes moved in a helpless sweep from his feet to the top of his dark head.

The lean, hungry look was more pronounced than it had been five years ago. He was harder; she looked into his eyes and saw blackness and nothing else. He might look the same but he wasn't, she realised as an icy chill slid down her spine.

'I am flattered that you remember me.' The mocking smile faded from his face and his words were terse and to the point. 'We need to talk.'

'Really?' She managed to inject a note of realistic surprise into her voice. 'Well, as much as I'd love to catch up,' she added with a smile of dazzling insincerity, 'right now is really not a good moment. I have a speaking engagement—' she gestured past him, hoping that he'd get the message she was not still the silly young woman desperately in love with him, so in love that she had sacrificed every principle she had lived by just to be with him '—and I need to speak with my PA rather urgently.'

'I think you want to make time for me.'

There was nothing covert about the threat in his words. 'Are you alone?'

She stiffened, sure that guilt was written all over her face as an image of her son's face covered in chocolate cake flashed into her head.

He couldn't know about him, but then, if he didn't, why was he here?

'My speaking engagement—'

'Your speaking engagement is tomorrow.'

Her long lashes flickered as she veiled her glance and her chin lifted another few notches in cool defiance, which she clung to with single-minded determination. It was the only thing standing between her and outright gibbering panic.

'I like to be prepared.' *This* was something she couldn't have prepared for if she'd had a year; it was something that was not meant to happen—ever. How could anyone have prepared her for opening the door and finding six feet four inches of Roman Bardales standing there...in *this* hotel of all places?

Her thoughts continued to race in panicky ever-decreasing circles.

Could this be a coincidence?

Him—here in this place—now?

Or was it something more…? It was just her guilty conscience talking, suggested the voice in her head. She ignored it. Guilt was something she lived with every day; it was the price she'd paid, and it was something you were meant to feel when you made the conscious decision to conceal your child's existence from his father, irrespective of the reasoning behind that choice.

Seeing Roman again made her certain that, from a purely selfish point of view, she had made the right decision. Having this man dipping in and out of her and Jamie's lives would have made it impossible for her to build any sort of existence without him—he was such an incredible force of nature.

It was a decision she had made for her unborn child, yet robbing a child of his father was not something you did lightly, and her eventual decision had come with the knowledge that she would never stop feeling guilty. But better surely to have no father than one who rejected you or, at best, acknowledged you with reluctance.

She wasn't sure which would be worse, but Marisa knew from personal experience that a child who had been deserted by a parent grew up thinking that it was somehow their fault, even when logic and a loving father in her case had told her otherwise. Not that her dad had ever bad-mouthed her mother; he had just said that motherhood was something she was not equipped to cope with.

She'd had the advantage of knowing that one parent could be enough. Her dad had been enough for her; sure, he wasn't perfect, but whatever his faults she had always known he loved her and that was what mattered.

Her baby would never doubt her love or be made to feel that he was not good enough so she had never faltered in the belief that, morality aside, she had done the right thing... All right, perhaps she'd faltered a little...more a stumble, really, and that had only been her hormones. After Jamie had been born, in the post-birth euphoria she had nearly changed her mind about telling Roman.

She'd been so blown away by Jamie, she'd thought he was so perfect how could anyone *not* want to be part of his life? She had wanted so much to share this feeling with Roman, it had seemed selfish not to, and when she'd fallen asleep staring at the life she had brought into the world it had all seemed so simple.

When she'd awoken the memories had resurfaced, bringing with them a deep sense of sadness. Roman was only going to be happy about the news he was a father in her dreams. He would not share her joy. How could he when he had felt strongly enough on the subject to make it a condition of his marriage proposal?

Marriage to him, he had warned her, would not involve children...and this was not something he was ever going to change his mind about. A *deal-breaker*, he had called it.

So she had made her decision and lived with it.

'I'm sorry but, no, I'm not going to invite you in. I prefer to leave the past in the past,' she said quietly, wondering if it would actually stay there.

'I just bet you do.'

Trying not to look worried, she didn't ask him what he meant by that because he might just tell her, and though she knew that some fights were inevitable, you could at least choose your own time and place to have them.

*Can we have a rain check on this conver-
sation? How does thirty years' time sound to
you?*

He arched a sardonic brow. 'Fine, then we
can discuss this out here if you prefer?'

She folded her arms across her chest in an
unconsciously protective gesture. 'I don't want
to talk to you at all.'

'Oh, by the way, my brother sends his love,
or he would have if he'd been in any condition
to talk when I last saw him.'

Marisa pressed one hand to her stomach and
the other shaking hand went to her mouth. 'He
told you.'

It wasn't a question but Roman responded
anyway.

'Rio came over with a sudden attack of conscience,' he remarked dryly, before adding in
a voice that was as hard as his eyes were cold,
'though it was a bit late in the day to matter.'

Without a word she turned around and went
back into her suite, expecting him to follow
her.

When the door closed behind him, she turned
back to face him. She could tell he wasn't quite
sure what to expect as she fixed him with a

direct amber stare. 'Sit down.' She gestured towards the brocade-covered sofa and heard herself ask with stiff formality, 'Can I get you anything to drink...tea?'

If there was a single thing she could have said that would have sounded more ludicrous in the circumstances she couldn't think of it.

His explosive expletive and the glare of incredulity did not come as a massive surprise. She pressed a hand to her throat where she could feel the ferocious beating of the pulse at the base of her neck.

'I think you're taking this lady of the manor stuff a bit too seriously.'

Marisa ignored his sneer and shrugged. 'Suit yourself.'

She glanced at his bruised knuckles.

'You fought with your brother over this?' She watched him place his uninjured hand over his bruised knuckles and her heart sank. 'You do know,' she began, her forehead creased with consternation, 'that your brother badly wanted to tell you.'

She had never wanted to come between the brothers but she had seen no other way. It wasn't until much later when Jamie had been given the all-clear that she had thought through the implications of putting Rio in that terrible position of keeping such a huge secret from his twin, but she had thought that so long as Roman never discovered what had happened it would be all right.

'But he didn't.'

'He wanted to tell you!' Marisa protested again.

Her defence of his twin only fed his anger. 'A conspiracy takes two at the very least.'

'It was my decision. We only had a casual relationship, after all, and not even a relationship in the real sense of the word, really—'

'I proposed to you! I wanted to get married! Admittedly I didn't know at that point you already had a husband, but proposing to you seems to suggest more than *casual* on my part, wouldn't you say?'

It was Marisa's turn to be angry. 'Why didn't I tell you about our baby? Oh, I don't know, Roman—how about the small print in your proposal?'

'What the hell are you talking about?'

Her fists clenched in reaction to his response, she shot to her feet, her anger energising her. 'You made it quite clear to me that if I did marry you there would be no children under *any* circumstances and you were not ever going to change your mind.'

A blank look spread across his face. 'I might have said something like that—'

'No, you said *exactly* that, so what would you have said if I'd come to you and told you I was pregnant, Roman? You'd have said, "Great, let's be a family," would you? Do me a favour, of course you wouldn't. You'd have told me to get rid of it.'

The accusation wiped all the colour from his face but, ignoring all the danger signs, she pushed on, the long-suppressed emotions spilling out of her.

'Jamie is only here because of me...you never even wanted him to exist.' Her flashing eyes dared him to contradict her, not that she allowed him the opportunity. There was a breathless passionate sincerity in her concluding words. 'But from the moment I knew he existed I *wanted* my baby.'

Her words rang with a truth that for a moment silenced him.

'We will never know what I'd have said or

done, will we? Because you didn't tell me. You let the world and presumably your poor sucker of a husband believe that the child was his.'

'Rupert never knew. I didn't realise that I was pregnant until after he...after he died.' She had put the tiredness down to the upheaval of Rupert's death, always expected, but in the end it had all happened very quickly, leaving her feeling dazed and alone. Theirs might not have been a marriage in the conventional sense but while Rupert was alive she had always known there was someone who cared about her. His support had not just been financial, but emotional. For a short time, probably the only time in her life, she'd had a security that she had always lacked, that she had secretly longed for.

Her first suspicion had come when she was sitting in the lawyer's office feeling nauseous. She had got so tired of sitting there nodding in response to statements couched in dry, technical legal terms and had asked wearily, 'But what does all that *mean*?'

'It means, Mrs Rayner, that you are a very wealthy woman.'

'But if he had you'd have passed my child

off as his, though I suppose that would have involved you sleeping with him first,' Roman jeered.

She felt her anger flare. 'You have no right to speak about Rupert like that. We had no secrets from one another, and if things had been different he would have made a fantastic father.'

'So you told him all about me, then?'

Her eyes slid from his for the first time. 'It wasn't the right time.' When she'd arrived back the evening of Roman's proposal the butler had greeted her at the door with the news that Rupert had had a very bad turn.

Rushing up the stairs to her husband's bedroom, she'd taken in at a glance his grey face and had immediately called an ambulance. How could she have offloaded her problems onto Rupert when he was so ill?

'Where is the child now?' Something flashed in his eyes. 'What do you call him? James or Alexander?'

'Jamie, and he is at home.' She hadn't even known the country estate in Sussex had existed until she'd inherited it after Rupert's death. Then it had seemed like the perfect place to bring up a child.

'So how often do you leave him?'

Resenting that he made her sound like some sort of absentee mother, she began to retort hotly and then stopped herself, realising she had been on the brink of explaining herself to him. 'Do you have a problem with working mothers?'

He blinked at finding she had neatly turned the tables on him. 'Of course I don't,' he retorted irritably.

'Actually, he has a very excellent nanny.'

'So where is home, exactly?'

'Sussex.'

'I want to see him.'

'Why?'

His brows met in a straight line above his dark eyes and he looked at her as though she had just asked the most ridiculous question on earth. 'Isn't it obvious? He is my son!'

'Biologically, yes, he is your son,' she agreed. 'But you're not his *father*—it takes more than DNA to be that. What do you want, Roman? To hear him call you Daddy or do you want him to appear in front of you on his best behaviour once or twice a year?'

'I want—' He paused and then went on

slowly, 'You have robbed me of nearly five years of his life so I think you owe me this.'

'And if I say no?' She already knew the answer to that, and if she hadn't, the expression in his liquid dark eyes and the ruthless smile on his face would have been confirmation.

'I will not permit you to say no. You owe me, Marisa.'

She pressed her fingers to her temple where needles of pain were telling her that a migraine was inevitable at this stage.

Another inevitability was that if she refused Roman access to Jamie he would only find another way. At least if she agreed to a meeting, she could control the situation. A quick glance at his profile made her realise that she was being overly optimistic.

'I owe *Jamie*, but I can see how you might feel that. So how about Friday?'

The offer made, she held her breath and waited…

'Tomorrow.'

'But I—'

'Your event is in the morning. Sussex is not Outer Mongolia, is it? I'll be there at two.'

CHAPTER FOUR

RUPERT HAD BOUGHT the Carolean manor and the surrounding acres as an investment. But to Marisa it was her home, maybe her first real one. She had never known where she was going to spend her holidays: a hotel suite in the South of France, a luxury penthouse in London or, when her father was down on his luck, not that she had realised it at the time, as a guest in one of her dad's friends' homes. She had slept on a lot of floors in her time.

She'd had some pretty bedrooms too over the years but she had learnt not to get too attached to them. She kept her important possessions, the ones that mattered to her, in an easily transportable tin for convenience, kept under whatever bed she was sleeping in.

She wanted Jamie's childhood to have the feeling of permanence she had always longed for, have the pets she could never have and the lasting friendships.

She'd moved into Rozens Manor when she was pregnant so this was the longest she had ever lived anywhere. The previous owner had renovated the house and outbuildings and Rupert hadn't touched them, not interested in putting his stamp on the place into which he had just installed a skeleton staff to maintain it.

After opening it up Marisa had put her own stamp on it instead, enjoying the process of refurbishment, but she had seen no reason to increase the number of staff already employed. The place was, in estate-agent speak, a small manageable estate, in as much as anywhere that had eight bedrooms, a dower house and converted stables could be termed *small*.

The only new member of staff was the nanny, who even in this enlightened age had raised a few eyebrows, and he was with Jamie in the garden now as she waited for Roman's arrival with the sort of enthusiasm normally reserved for the flu.

She had given everyone else a day off. The local tongues had wagged enough when she'd employed a male nanny, but while gossip was inevitable, and would probably not be confined to the local community when Roman appeared, there was no point inviting it, especially this early.

Roman was obviously keen to stake his claim but, given that children had never been part of his plan, who knew how he would react when faced with the reality of parenthood, a reality that he had been so deadly determined to avoid? Marisa had no idea what his reasons were for not wanting children, and though she was ready to accept that people *could* change, this situation wasn't the same as discovering you liked broccoli after a lifetime of avoidance—this was *fundamental*.

Roman *said* he wanted to be part of his son's life but could she trust this knee-jerk reaction? She could wear contact lenses and have blue eyes, but they wouldn't *really* be blue. Roman said he wanted to be a father…hell, he *demanded* it, and he might even think he meant it, but would he really once reality hit?

There wasn't a single conclusion to the incessant questions that had kept her up into the small hours and none of the scenarios Marisa had dreamt up were ones that made her happy. She didn't want Roman in their lives, but for

Jamie's sake she didn't want him to reject his son either.

One hand pressed to the coat of arms above the fireplace of the long-dead people who had built this place, she was staring deep into the bowl of hydrangeas that filled the carved stone recess when she heard a car door slamming.

Marisa swallowed and tugged nervously at the roll-collar neckline of the fine-sleeved navy cashmere top she had teamed with a pair of pale blue linen cut-off trousers and soft leather ballerina slip-ons, because she hadn't wanted to give the impression she was trying *too* hard.

She was going to be cool, casual but in control, and they were going to play by her rules because this was about Jamie.

She closed her eyes for the count of ten before squaring her shoulders at the distinctive sound of gravel crunching under a purposeful rapid stride. The sound spurred her into action because for some reason at that moment it felt important that she open the door, not respond to his knock demanding entry.

The soles of her shoes made no noise on the flagged floor as she made a dash to the door that was flanked by two carved stone lions and, rather more practically, a wellington rack. The massive metal-banded door complete with the original seventeenth-century key was heavy to open so she was glad she'd left it slightly ajar.

A last-minute smoothing down of her hair and a conscious effort to iron out the frown lines of tension on her brow and she pushed the door further open, her smile of welcome fighting with the wariness in her eyes.

Roman paused as the door swung open revealing the slim figure who presumably had been standing behind it. He took a deep breath and held it because she looked so... His thoughts tailed off. He had no word for it or for the reaction her physical presence had on his nervous system.

He settled for *elegant*, ignoring the voice inside his head that scorned this cop-out. It was true, even drenched to the skin in mud-splattered clothes and with her hair plastered to her skull that first time they'd met, she had still radiated an elegance that was simply innate and no more contrived than being left-handed was.

Combined with her earthy sexuality, it was a devastating combination.

He liked things of beauty—who didn't?—and even if there was more sex than aesthetics involved in the heat that streaked through him, settling in his groin, he knew there was no danger of him mistaking this reaction for anything more significant.

He had moved on.

Which did not mean he could deny the mind-sapping effect her physical presence had on him. He could enjoy the way she moved, though *enjoy*, he conceded, was perhaps the wrong word for the fascination her most mundane actions exerted and the inevitable gut-punch of raw hunger that followed—but there was absolutely no question of him doing anything about it. And, more importantly, no question of him mistaking what had been excellent, actually *exceptional*, sex for some sort of deeper bond between them.

They were going to have contact, it was inevitable, so in the meantime he was just going to have to suck it up, until this thing burnt itself out. He had never known it not to, so he was confident that in time this would too.

Cool, casual and controlled, Marisa felt none of the above, but then it had never been an exactly realistic expectation. Maybe there would come a time when she could, if not relax, at least feel less...exposed around Roman, but that day was a long way off yet, so she decided to settle for guarded.

Employing her lashes to conceal the compulsive sweep of her gaze as it moved up his lean body, she noted he had opted for his version of casual today, wearing the black jeans that emphasised the length of his own legs and the power of his muscular thighs, his leather jacket open to reveal a summer-weight fine-wool tailored sweater.

His chiselled jaw was clean-shaven and his dark hair was shorter than it had been the previous day, the sharp, close cut emphasising the stark perfection of his bone structure, the overall effect one of *maleness*, effortless power and exclusivity.

Fragments of their conversation the previous day had been floating through her head ever since, all unresolved issues, question marks and guilt carried over to today, the weight of it all making it feel as if she were walking around in a heavy overcoat.

The couple of painkillers she had swallowed earlier had done nothing to relieve the headache; like the guilt, it was probably permanent, she decided dully.

Pushing through the negativity, she forced another smile. 'Hello, you found us.'

'You are not exactly hidden.'

Before she could follow up with an invitation for him to come in or work out the edge in his words he stepped past her into the hallway. Many first-time visitors stepping over the threshold were charmed by the light interior, commenting on the original flagged floor, the flowers set in the inglenook or the massive age-blackened beam above it.

Roman didn't look charmed, but then he was a Bardales and his horses probably lived somewhere grander than this.

'So nice to see you,' she drawled sardonically as he walked into the middle of the hallway and turned around to face her. Her nervous system was struggling to adjust to his presence—actually, she was just struggling, full stop.

He either ignored the sarcasm or he didn't notice it. 'I just drove straight in here.' Hands held out in front of him, palms facing upwards, he gave an incredulous shrug and waited for her explanation.

Not sure what sort of response he clearly wanted, instead she watched the muscles in his jaw quiver. She had no idea why he was angry...very angry, so she limited her reply to a cautious little—

'Oh?'

'Do you actually have *any* security?' He reached out and touched the door key, original and solid, seeming to imply her entire attitude to modern security was lacking.

Whatever she had imagined he was so wound up over it was not this—*security*? Had he expected to pass a guard checkpoint with metal detectors? To see guard dogs patrolling the perimeter of the small estate set in a leafy backwater where the crime figures probably skewed the national statistics?

'Security as in...?' His expression made her rush on before he exploded. 'Well, nothing beyond the basic, but we have a very good alarm system. It's only five years old.'

'A ten-year-old could break in here.'

His scorn made her lips tighten. 'Well, the insurance firm were more than satisfied.' When they'd given her their quote their only stipulation was that she keep all her jewellery in a bank vault, and that was no problem because Marisa couldn't imagine herself wearing any of the elaborate, mostly Victorian stuff she'd inherited from Rupert. She'd have given it to a surviving family member had there been one. 'There isn't really anything of enormous value here.' Not since she had lent Rupert's collection of modern paintings to a grateful gallery. They were not really to her taste and the artwork that had replaced them was an eclectic mix of mostly local artists, and certainly not valuable.

'How about our son?'

Her eyes widened as the colour seeped with dramatic speed from her face, leaving two bands of angry stain along the curves of her cheekbones.

She was shaking with fury…just… Well, how dared he walk in here and start implying she couldn't care for her own son? She inhaled sharply, then fixed him with a molten gold glare and folded her arms across her chest as if to contain the emotions she was struggling to control.

'So you think the best way to work out an amicable arrangement between us is to walk in here and start throwing around accusations? You are here as a guest. I do not answer to you. I have been taking care of Jamie for four and a half years...' Unconsciously her hands went to her stomach as she pulled in a tense breath. 'Actually, even longer than that. He is everything to me and has been ever since the moment I knew I'd conceived and I would—' She suddenly stopped. 'Why on earth am I defending myself to you?' she muttered half to herself.

She didn't add the words, *To someone who hasn't been here and didn't even want a child*, but she really wanted to. He clearly read the sentiment shining in the contempt of her glare, because he spread his hands, his long fingers extended in a pacifying gesture.

'I might have overreacted somewhat.'

Partly mollified by his unexpected climb-down, even if it had come across as reluctant rather than humble, she gave a slightly hysterical laugh from her dry throat, which she covered with a fake cough that quickly turned into a genuine one.

'Are you contagious?'

'You can't control a cough...' she retorted, reading irritation in his stiff expression. An image floated unbidden into her head of Roman, his face a mask of carnal need, curved over her, his knees between her thighs and his hands curled around her wrists. It was so real she could have sworn in the split second before she banished it that she could feel his warm breath on her face.

'Shall we start again?' he suggested.

Her fingernails inscribing crescent moons into the soft palms of her hands, she nodded and made an effort to unclench, everywhere.

'I know this must be hard for you—' she began, only to be spoken over immediately.

'I do not require your sympathy.'

She sucked in a breath and glared at him standing there, hauteur and disdain stamped all over his patrician face. 'Fine, then assume you don't have it,' she countered, her eyes flashing gold fire before she pulled her protective cloak of coolness around her once more. 'For the record, it's a very quiet area.' She made sure there was nothing whatever placatory about her statement. 'Jamie is never alone; if I'm not there, his nanny is.'

She could tell he was thinking that a nanny did not seem adequate protection against an individual intent on kidnap or whatever it was he was imagining would happen, but he clamped his lips over this observation instead.

'We really do have a good security system and the estate wall is several feet of solid granite,' she continued, 'but I want Jamie to have as normal a childhood as possible and he is perfectly safe here.'

She could almost see him fighting back another retort but she was too stressed to see the funny side of this—*was* there even a funny side to see?

'I never intended to imply—' he began.

She cut across him in a flat voice and dug her hands into the pockets of the trousers that were tailored enough to show off the narrowness of her waist and the shapely length of her thighs and slim calves.

'But you did.'

It was a relief when his intense gaze left her

face and she took the opportunity to breathe, *really* breathe. She could only hope that this would get easier because the effort of maintaining the illusion that she was in charge of this situation... No, she *was* in charge, she told herself, but it was still exhausting.

Yet it was essential. If she lowered her guard she was convinced Roman would bulldoze through her to get to Jamie, and this, she reminded herself, ashamed that she even needed to, was all about Jamie and what was best for him.

If Roman got the idea that she was a doormat, he would keep trying to walk all over her. She unconsciously lifted her chin; in her defence it was easy to forget who was in charge when you were in a room with a man who dominated this and any other space he happened to be in.

'Can I get you anything...tea, coffee?'

The polite question brought his wandering gaze back to her face as he slung her an incredulous *Are you joking?* look.

'You can get me my son.'

It wasn't just the possessive inflection but the underlying hungry need in his voice that sent a fresh trickle of unease down her stiff spine. As the tension climbed back into her shoulders, she watched his eyes search the space behind her as though he expected to see Jamie suddenly appear.

'Jamie is outside in the garden,' she explained with a sense of calm she was certainly not feeling. 'I want to get a few ground rules sorted first.'

Astonishment flashed across his face. 'You...?' She could almost see the quivering line as he reeled in the rest of his response and stood there directing his fierce black stare at her, presumably waiting for her to fall apart or maybe at his feet begging forgiveness. He might have stepped out of the boardroom in recent years but he had lost none of the arrogance she remembered...if she had ever needed a reminder that he was no laid-back thriller writer. Roman was a maverick, the man who made the rules, not the man who followed them.

She moistened her lips with the tip of her tongue and waited as long as she could bear before she blurted out, 'So are you all right with that?' The tiny flash of something close to admiration in his dark eyes before he dropped his gimlet gaze might only have existed in her imagination, but her sense of triumph was real as she silently chalked up an invisible line in the air.

Her tiny burst of optimism vanished as she contemplated her immediate future stretching out in front of her like a winding road with no end in sight.

God, it was depressing! *Somehow* she would have to slot Roman into their lives, but as she regarded his tall, imposing person through the shade of her lashes, she felt her heart sink even lower. He really wasn't a person who slotted into any neat space; he dominated every environment. She repressed a sigh and thought wistfully of her life a few short days ago. It had been neat and ordered and her stomach *hadn't*... She hadn't *felt*... Her fluttering gaze lingered tremblingly for a split second too long on the sculpted firm contours of his overtly sensual mouth and her insides dissolved hotly as lust suddenly paralysed her ability to think *anything*.

'So what are *your* ground rules?' His voice was low and disconcertingly expressionless as he pushed the words past his even, clenched white teeth, but at least it gave her the impetus to drag herself free of the sensual vortex that had held her immobile for a few shaming moments.

This was what she had been trying not to think about: the fact, inescapable and shameful, that after all that had happened she was still disastrously attracted to Roman... No, *attracted* was an insipid word to describe her physical response to him, which in the past she had thought of as a form of temporary insanity.

Except it wasn't temporary!

She had been avoiding it by focusing on the practicalities involved with bringing him into Jamie's life. The irony of this scenario was wedged like a lead weight against her breastbone. He clearly resented her being in control when in actuality she had not felt less in control...at least of her own body for...well, actually ever since she had left his hotel room more than five years ago.

As the pounding in her head stepped up its painful tempo her aggravation and seething frustration exploded into speech. 'I really wish you wouldn't take everything so personally, Roman! I'm not trying to make a point, but actually, if you want to look at it that way, they *are* my rules.

'If you want to be *any* part of Jamie's life...' She paused, wondering if he actually knew what he wanted in practical terms, but not sure she actually wanted to know. 'I'm genuinely not trying to be awkward. *I'm—*' Her waving hand gesture and helpless shoulder shrug begged his understanding. When there was no crack in his stony façade she shook her head. 'I'm trying to avoid a difficult situation. He is only four and I don't want him confused, so you can't rush him. He needs to get to know you before we tell him who you are.'

Roman's head reared back as though she'd struck him. 'You're protecting him from me?'

The same way his mother had tried to protect him and Rio from their father.

'You need to be patient, Roman.' She sighed. 'You can't expect him to just...'

'Love me.'

A short, strained silence followed this interruption.

'That wasn't what I was about to say,' she

said quietly. She gnawed gently on her full lower lip, the action causing his eyes to drift in that direction, pausing on the lush plumpness that bore the imprint of her teeth. 'I just wanted to warn...' He stiffened and she held up both hands. 'Oh, for heaven's sake, this is like walking on eggshells! This is hard enough without you being so damned touchy. I'm just trying to say—if you'll let me?'

Their eyes connected and after a short pause one corner of his mouth lifted. 'Go ahead...' He opened his hand in invitation.

'I'm just trying to warn you not to expect too much too soon. We haven't really discussed just how we're going to do this, but I don't want you to have unrealistic expectations.'

'You're trying to warn me not to expect him to love me on sight. I'm not an idiot, Marisa.'

'I think we should take things slowly.'

A nerve clenched in his lean cheek. He'd waited five years, he told himself; a few more days would not matter.

'In a few months when—'

'*Months!*'

Marisa lowered her gaze, seeing no point in pushing things any further. 'Let's just play it by ear, shall we?' His silence was better than an argument and she decided to interpret his grim expression as a yes. 'He's playing outside—this way.' She gestured to the open door to their left.

For a split second she thought he was not going to react to her invitation, and she allowed herself a little sigh of relief when he did.

Conscious of his towering presence, in every sense of the word, she led the way through the doorway to the rear of the house past what had once been a dairy and was now a boot room. She unlatched the closed portion of the stable door that led out to the kitchen garden, where gravel paths wove their way through a geometric arrangement of raised beds bursting with a variety of leafy green vegetables, herbs and soft fruit, each bordered by neatly trimmed box hedging.

'That one is Jamie's garden,' she said with a proud smile as they passed one of the raised beds that stood out from the other well-tended beds with their straight lines and leafy growth because there were no straight lines in sight, just patches of seedlings poking their way through the ground in artistic swirls, and seed packets tied to sticks fluttering in the breeze.

She turned her head to explain to Roman how much Jamie loved to watch things grow and his fascination with creepy-crawlies, and caught a look on his lean face as he followed her gaze and registered the swirls of green, that brought a lump to her throat and an ache of unexpected empathy to her heart. She looked away quickly but was left with a feeling that she had suddenly intruded on a very private moment.

When she turned back, the mixture of longing and loss was gone as he righted a wooden marker that said *trees*, the wobbly letters in green marker pen sloping, the *s* back to front.

'He calls broccoli *trees*,' she explained as he straightened up and dusted his hands on the seat of his immaculate jeans, causing a stab of longing to vibrate through her body, illustrating the danger of allowing empathy for him to breach her defences.

She had built a life that was stable and secure, for her and for Jamie, who'd had enough trauma in his short life to last several lifetimes. There had to be a way of allowing Roman access to him without disrupting what they had, and that wouldn't happen if she couldn't get her hormones under control.

She looked away and felt a fleeting stab of nostalgia for the days when she had imagined she was not someone who was particularly interested in sex. All it had taken was for Roman to appear on her horizon to blow that comforting theory completely out of the water.

'When he was…ill I promised him a garden. I thought he'd forget but—' she gave a rueful laugh '—he didn't, so don't go making any promises you can't keep because he'll hold you to them.'

Roman frowned. 'Very subtle.'

The sardonic rejoinder brought a sting of colour to her cheeks.

'Next you'll be telling me a child is for life, not just for Christmas. So is telling him lies prohibited or is lying by omission allowed?'

Roman watched her flush again as the jibe hit home, but it didn't make him feel particularly good.

She sighed.

'I'll tell Jamie you're a friend.'

He hid his reaction beneath his heavy half-lowered lids.

'So you'll lie to him again.' His head tilted to a mocking quizzical angle. 'Or are we friends?'

The mockery stung. Marisa knew they could never be friends...and she hated that the acknowledgment, quite illogically, made her sad.

People who had been lovers did stay friends but she assumed those people had things in common besides sex. The only thing they had in common besides sleeping together was Jamie. Without Jamie, Roman would not be here and she would not be... She took a deep breath and dragged her hand across the smooth hair that was moulded to her head like a shiny cap. She was skirting around the real elephant in the room, which was the complicated confusion of her feelings, the buzz in her bloodstream. She didn't want Roman here, so why did she feel more alive than she had in a long time?

'So you're all right with that?' she threw back with more than a hint of challenge.

The tightening of his jaw was a lot less casual than his shrug. 'Do I have a choice?'

She said nothing as she turned away, pointing to a gate in the low stone wall that ran down the length of the kitchen garden. 'This way.'

CHAPTER FIVE

THE STRIP OF WOODLAND was carpeted with snowdrops in spring and later bluebells but now in midsummer the undergrowth was tall and thick enough to scratch the legs of a little boy wearing shorts.

Jamie's yell of 'Not fair' drifted across the intervening space. He was fifty yards away on the other side of the small paddock where a goalpost had been erected, but Marisa could see that the blood oozing from a cut on Jamie's knee was not a scratch, at least in her head.

She took a deep breath and talked herself away from what she visualised as the panic ledge in her head. There had been a time in the not so distant past when she would have reacted to the sight of a grazed knee with full-blown drama; it was always a fight to repress her maternal protective instincts but she was getting there.

Wrapping Jamie up in cotton wool would

have made her life a lot easier but she had recognised it wouldn't be good for him so she made an effort to allow him the rough and tumble that any little boy enjoyed.

Her own fight to control her instincts had distracted her for a split second from the man who was walking a few steps behind her.

The sound of his muffled exclamation brought her head around just as he released a low rush of words in his native Spanish. She had no idea what they meant but it was hard to hear the painfully raw intonation without feeling a stab of empathy for his shocked reaction.

Looking at the expression stamped on his lean features, an expression as raw as his words and filled with a kind of painful longing, made her throat ache; swallowing, she looked away.

The father of her child might be a virtual stranger to her outside the bedroom but every instinct she had told her that he would hate for anyone to witness anything that he would consider a weakness.

'Apparently he has excellent hand-eye coordination,' she said to fill the growing screaming silence and give him time to recover himself.

When he did speak it was clear that she wasn't going to be getting any appreciation for her sensitivity.

'So who the hell is *that*?'

Marisa's head turned in response to his snarled question, the verbal equivalent of what she imagined a wolf's growl would sound like.

Her sense of impending doom deepened as she took in the rigid lines on his scowling face, but now it was mingled with exasperation.

'Your son,' she said, delivering a tight fake smile in response to his accusing glare.

'Do not be cute with me, Marisa.'

Her lips tightened. He might not like being on the receiving end of warnings but he appeared to have zero problem issuing them. Her indignation soared. Here was she, bending over backwards to make this as painless as possible for everyone, and all he could do was—

She heaved a deep restorative breath before tossing her head, causing several strands of shiny flaxen hair to escape the ponytail on the nape of her slim neck.

'I am never cute.' You could not be *cute* when you were a whisper short of five foot eleven. 'I assume you're referring to—' But then she paused as he wasn't just referring, he was positively glaring! 'That's Ashley.'

'And just who is Ashley?' Roman growled back, his eyes fixed on the rear view of the tall male who was kicking a ball back to his son...*his son*! The emotion swelled in his chest as his gaze transferred once more to the child with stick-thin legs who squealed with laughter as he kicked the ball past the man and then punched the air.

'Not fair, I wasn't ready!' the young blond man yelled back.

'Do you often leave our son in the care of your boyfriends?'

She blinked, her astonishment genuine, but it swiftly turned to annoyance. Eyes flaring, she folded her arms tightly across her chest. 'Ashley is Jamie's nanny.' Her chin lifted a defiant notch as she fixed him with a narrow-eyed glare. 'And what business of yours would it be if he was my boyfriend?' she challenged, thinking this was rich coming from someone who had a partiality for scantily clad blondes.

Roman spun around. *'Nanny?'* he echoed, fixing on the relevant part of her retort before his eyes and his brain got snagged on the sight of silky strands of pale hair shining against her dark jumper. The image was the catalyst that took him straight back to a time and place when that hair was longer and tangled, drifting across his chest as she sat astride him, the feathery light contact sending electrical surges along his nerve endings, before the caress was replaced by the touch of her lips.

The effort of escaping the erotic images before he was sucked back into the past brought a sheen of sweat to his brow, and his fingers clenched as he dragged in a mind-clearing lungful of oxygen.

Focus, man, think...he ordered himself.

The problem was, the thoughts in question involved another man playing with his son, his son looking up trustingly into another man's face and laughing.

Roman realised he seriously hated the thought of that man being more than Marisa's employee. From a mental file in his head of similar incidents came the memory of a scene, of his father driving them home after dinner, cross-examining his mother just because she had smiled at a waiter. She had flirted with the man, he'd accused, and he was sure she had given him her phone number.

They had sat there, he and Rio, and listened as their father had called their mother names that no man should call a woman. As children all they could do was kick the back of their father's seat in protest to try to make him stop. No longer a child, he would do so much more if he heard similar abuse now.

He would not be that man.

'I didn't realise there were any male nannies.' It was a rational observation, and he could have added that in his opinion nannies did not look as though they hit the gym on a daily basis before they ran out into the morning surf.

Marisa resisted the childish impulse to stamp her feet. It wasn't even what he'd said, it was the *way* he'd said it, his attitude of teeth-grating certainty that by simply saying something it made it so.

'Have you never heard of equality?' she enquired sweetly and earned herself another glare. 'Or do you think women have the ex-

clusive rights on *caring* for children?' she said
with blighting scorn, seeing no reason to admit
that it hadn't exactly been her own enlightened
thinking that had made her shortlist Ashley,
because until he had walked through the door
and her PA had leaned across and breathed,
'Wow, can he be my nanny?' she hadn't even
realised that Ashley was a man.

He had been the last interviewee, she remembered, and she'd been ready to give up,
as none of the other well-qualified candidates
had seemed a good fit. Probably because she
hadn't really wanted them to be, she thought
wryly. She hadn't wanted a mother substitute;
she was Jamie's mum.

She'd been the problem, not them, or at
least the fact that she didn't want a nanny, she
needed a nanny. The bad case of flu that had
meant she literally couldn't get out of bed for
a week—and, worse, had to keep away from
Jamie because she couldn't risk exposing him
to the virulent bug—had proved that.

It was times like that it really hit home to
her what it meant to be a single parent with
no husband to step into the breach. She had
no family ready to rush to help out in emer-

gencies either... At least she was one of the lucky ones who had enough money to pay for staff to help her, who had gone way beyond the call of duty, so Jamie was being well cared for, but it meant that she was imposing on people who she was sure would have preferred to be spending time with their own families.

Had she taken to Ashley so quickly because he wasn't a threat to her relationship with Jamie—he was not a mother substitute? She couldn't swear hand on heart that it hadn't been a factor but he was a good fit regardless, at least until Jamie started school full-time, or, to be more precise, the month before school started, which was when Ash was due to go travelling for a year before he started his university course next autumn, debt-free.

She really admired the young man's practicality, the fact he had put his ambition to be an architect on hold and got a childcare qualification first so he could earn some money before taking up a university place and also had a way of earning his keep while he was there.

'You kept very quiet about him,' Roman observed tautly, interrupting her thoughts.

She shook her head in genuine bewilderment. 'Was I quiet?' He made it sound as if she'd deliberately not told him. 'I'm pretty sure I mentioned him.'

'That Jamie had a nanny, yes, but not that he was a *he*.'

Her lips tightened. 'I didn't think it was relevant, because it isn't.'

'So no one ever comments on it?'

Her eyes slid from his. 'Oh, for God's sake, what is your problem?'

'I don't have a problem,' Roman denied, knowing he was lying.

Her delicate brows lifted. 'Yes, it really shows.'

Her laugh brought Roman's teeth together so hard he could feel them grate. It wasn't caring men that Roman had a problem with, it was the strong possibility, no, more like the *probability* that he was not one of them, that this quality was something you couldn't learn. You either had it, like the guy currently playing with his son, or you didn't.

Did Marisa admire this guy's *caring* qualities or was it his muscles she was interested in? Recognising that this less than charitable thought yet again came straight out of his own father's playbook did not improve his mood one little bit.

'I don't have a problem with male nannies.' He had no problems with male *anything*, he just had a problem with this particular guy, who was quite obviously being a great role model for *his* son, but he was not—absolutely *not*—jealous.

He was not that man; he was not his father.

His jaw clamped, the white line around his lips standing out stark against his tan. *Dios*, yes, he was!

This reaction was the reason he had spent his life avoiding caring enough to become a monster like his father. Only twice in his life had he allowed himself to care and each time—

He closed his eyes momentarily to cut out the sight of his child listening attentively to something the blond guy was saying to him. In fact, he was hanging on every syllable.

He wanted his son to look at him the way he was looking at his nanny.

The shock of that vibrated though him, jarring like a discordant off-key note. He had accepted that he had a son, accepted that the child was his responsibility, but he had not anticipated having these feelings for him, or that they would be instantaneous.

He hadn't even registered the young guy who was the focus of his envy initially, because his focus had been so completely on the child running across the grass on his skinny little legs.

Knowing he had a child, he'd discovered, was an entirely different thing from actually seeing him, no longer a theoretical son, but a real flesh and blood kid. One with tangled hair, a shiny sweat-slicked face and blood from a graze on his knee staining one sock.

The impact was almost physical. Roman felt as if someone had just landed an unprotected direct hit on his solar plexus, the invisible blow causing the breath to leave his chest in a gasp as a nameless aching feeling rushed to fill the vacuum that was left.

It was not hard to recognise a game-changing moment when it hit you in the face, and this was it. Duty had brought him here but this totally unanticipated feeling was going to keep him here, was going to keep him in his son's life.

'Mum!'

Roman watched the child's face light up as he spotted his mother, who began waving back.

'Watch what I can do—it's really cool skills!' he yelled as he balanced the football on his knee for at least two seconds before picking it up and waiting for the applause.

It came right on cue, and the sight of Marisa's smiling face, her enthusiastic clapping, her cheery thumbs up, shook loose some fresh nameless emotion deep inside Roman that he didn't want to acknowledge.

'Excellent skills!' she approved.

He turned his head sharply, remembering again his brother's expression as his twin had held his own small daughter close to his chest. It had been a faint echo compared to what Roman felt now. *Envy, loss, regret...* None of them were legitimate responses for a man who had never wanted children.

He still believed in the reasoning behind his decision not to have children. The facts had not changed, and it was a decision he would make again if he had been able to. Why run the risk of passing on the tainted genes, replicate painful history, inflict the sort of emotional damage on his child his own father had on him and Rio?

But that option was gone; it was firmly in the past. In the present he had a son, that was the reality he was dealing with now, and it came with an unaccustomed sense of inadequacy he was struggling to deal with.

So far he had succeeded in not acknowledging the fear he knew was lurking underneath the anger, but it had been much easier to focus on confronting Marisa about her actions than acknowledging it.

If it gets tough, you can always fall back on blaming her for everything, sneered the contemptuous voice in his head,

Roman knew about this *visceral* connection, this blood calling to blood... He glanced down and saw that his white-knuckled fist was clenched against his chest, and self-consciously he allowed it to fall back to his side. Now he knew why his brother had finally decided to break his silence about Jamie's existence, break his promise to Marisa. Because of this *feeling* that was tearing Roman apart right now—Rio knew what it felt like to be a father.

To banish the surge of empathy, because he really didn't want to stop being angry with his twin, and he definitely didn't want to be *grateful* to him, Roman replaced his brother's face with a mental image of their own father, who had rarely noticed his sons were alive unless he'd wanted to use them to get to their mother. They'd only ever been a useful tool or an inconvenience to him.

The voice in his head urging caution was almost drowned out by the overwhelming surge of paternal feeling that had just materialised out of nowhere.

There were still very good reasons why this child would be so much better off without Roman in his life, but he knew he was not selfless enough to keep a safe distance from him.

'He is a big soccer fan.'

Roman didn't respond to Marisa, but she could feel the emotions emanating from him across the distance between them. She slid a glance up at him. His profile was as rigid as his body language; everything about him was *clenched*.

No wonder he looked tense—this had to

be his nightmare scenario. His apparently in-grained sense of duty was probably the only thing stopping him from heading for the near-est exit at high speed.

Would it be a problem if he did?

Not for her, she told herself. Her life would be a lot easier without Roman in it, a lot more vanilla and safe, which obviously would be a good thing. She could live without drama; she could live without sex.

Always good to wait to be asked before re-fusing it, Marisa.

Feeling the heat climb into her cheeks, she retracted her gaze, retreating under the shade of her lashes. Any sympathy she might feel for Roman—the man whose antipathy for chil-dren was presumably strong enough to make not having them a condition of a marriage pro-posal, and who had then found himself a fa-ther—was tempered by her main concern for Jamie and the effect the sudden appearance of a father in his life would have on him.

Roman was here now, but who was to say that he wouldn't want to opt out at some fu-ture point, a point when Jamie would know he had been rejected? Having something and losing it was a lot different from not missing what you'd never had. A feeling she knew all too well, she mused grimly, reflecting on her blissful ignorance before Roman had taught her how to enjoy her own body and his!

This is about Jamie, Marisa.

'So is he any good at what he does?' Roman asked, resenting the ease with which Ashley was making his son laugh as he watched the interaction, the easy rapport between man and boy.

He made it look easy, and Rio had made it look easy too. To Roman it did not seem easy, it seemed—

He didn't even know what the thing he lacked was, he concluded with a burst of self-contempt for his sheer cluelessness.

Could you learn how to be a good father? Just the basics—or if you couldn't learn to be a good father, then at the very least one that did no harm.

Roman had achieved much that people would envy in his life, but it had all come so easily to him. At that moment he would have exchanged every single thing he had achieved for the nanny's ability to be so relaxed with a child, or rather this particular child...*his* child.

It was her little artificial laugh that broke the downward spiral of his depressing internal dialogue. His glance slewed her way; there was no amusement on her face to match the laugh.

She was standing there ramrod stiff, her chin lifted to a militant angle as she fixed him with a narrow-eyed glare of icy challenge.

'What exactly is *that* meant to mean?'

In the past Marisa had taken the teasing comments about Ashley and the inevitable double entendres when friends and other mothers had met the handsome young addition to her household in good part. None of it was malicious, although it got a bit tiresome at times, but nothing she couldn't handle. If laughter didn't close down the subject she had a whole list of comical comebacks at her disposal.

Somehow she didn't feel like laughing now.

Roman's brows tugged together as he studied her hot, antagonistic face.

'I mean...' he began, then stopped, comprehension spreading across his face as his gaze flashed between the young man and Marisa, something kicking hard in his gut as he joined the dots and watched a picture form that explained her defensive attitude.

Was it possible he had jumped to the *right* conclusion after all? Had she given herself to this youth with as much passion as she had him? Had Ashley watched the concentration on her face as she fought to reach her climax? Had he felt…? Damping the sweat he could feel beading on his upper lip with a slightly shaking hand, he clamped down on the feverish speculation that would only feed the ever-present ache of wanting something he couldn't have, something that, even after everything that had happened between them, he still had zero control over.

Zero control was a hard thing to admit for a man who prided himself on his, be it on the rock face, delivering a daily word count or picking apart an argument that had stupidity written all over it without losing his temper.

But what she made him feel was beyond his powers of self-deception. Far better to own a weakness than run away from it or get too hung up over it.

No point overcomplicating the situation. He was feeling something he didn't want to feel;

wanting her and not being able to have her was a kind of torture, but, he told himself grimly, he could live with it, treat it like any other chemical imbalance in his brain.

'Interesting reaction,' he drawled. 'Have I touched a nerve?'

His sarcasm freed her from the embarrassment. 'Ashley lives in the flat over the stables. He is only a boy.' The moment Marisa said it she wanted to take it back, furious with herself for bothering to explain. Roman could think what he liked.

'I was a boy once too and a few years' age gap never seemed like an obstacle to me.'

'I just bet it didn't!' she snapped back. 'But before you start getting nostalgic about all the notches on your bedpost—' she diverted her gaze to the game of football '—for the record and because you clearly judge others by your very low standards, I am not *sleeping* with Ashley.' She shrugged and added, 'Yet.'

'Is that meant to make me jealous?'

'I thought you already were.'

When he didn't reply, she turned and lifted her gaze to Roman's face, catching the tail end of a puzzling expression that vanished so quickly she decided she had imagined it. 'Shall I call Jamie over?'

'That's what I'm here for.'

Marisa waved and called out, and with obvious reluctance Jamie came trotting over, his tall nanny following behind, the football in his hands.

'Jamie, this is someone I want you to meet. His name is Mr—'

'Roman.'

'This is Roman and he has come to have tea with us.'

'Tea...' The lower lip came out. 'I don't want tea. I wanna play football with Ash and afterwards—'

'Enough football for one day, mate. It's my afternoon off,' the nanny interjected.

Hands clenched at his sides, the little boy aimed a kick at the football that Ashley had placed on the ground. It went sailing away before he swung back to the trio of adults, looking mutinous, though most of his ire seemed aimed at Roman. 'But that's not fair...'

'Not fair is expecting someone else to pick up your toys...' Ashley nodded towards the ball that had sailed into a bed of flowers. 'Go get it, and I'll see you on Monday.'

Roman watched, the empty space in his chest aching, as the child gave a deep sigh and trotted off across the expanse of green grass.

'He has quite a kick.'

Roman turned towards the nanny. Somehow the word did not fit a six-foot-three man with a tattoo on his neck, even one as innocuous as a rose with fallen petals.

He said nothing, seeing that the younger man was standing beside Marisa now. Clearly they'd been talking but he'd been too focused on his son to register the conversation. His eyes narrowed as he noticed how close the two were standing together, their posture, their body language revealing how comfortable they were with one another. He inhaled sharply. *Jealous*, she had said.

He made himself exhale again. She might not be sleeping with this particular man but it would be naïve of him to imagine that a woman of her sexuality had spent the last few years living the life of a nun.

Ashley made his goodbyes and turned to Roman with a polite, 'Nice to meet you.'

Roman could only manage a nod in response, his glacial stare still in place, and he could see Marisa heave a sigh of exasperation before she added, 'Enjoy your long weekend, Ash.'

'I will.'

Roman watched as the nanny jogged off and out of view.

'That was rude.'

One dark brow lifted. 'If that was rude, what would you call not telling a man he is the father of your child?' In his head the retort had not sounded quite so brutal but the result was the same.

All the animation went out of her face, and she stiffened, seeming to almost physically shrink back from him.

He should have felt satisfied at her reaction but her discomfort afforded him surprisingly little pleasure.

With clenched hands set on her hips, she turned to face him, her luminous eyes calm but determined in her pale face.

'If you imagine you can close down any conversation by playing the victim card, I think you should go for another strategy,' she advised him tartly.

And he had started to feel a glimmer of sympathy for her. Stung, he snapped back, *'Victim?'*

On another occasion Roman's expression of outraged incredulity would have made Marisa laugh but at that moment laughter was beyond her. This was an impossible situation, which she couldn't see getting better any time soon, but for Jamie's sake she had to try.

'If you're always going to resent me, fine, that is your choice, but if you actually do want to form any sort of relationship with our son—'

'A child should know who his father is.'

Her brow creased. 'That wasn't what I asked,' she threw back, annoyed by his politician's response.

Was he saying that he didn't want a relationship with Jamie, that he didn't want to be part of Jamie's life after all? She shouldn't be surprised and she definitely shouldn't be disappointed…after all, it would make her life a hell of a lot easier.

As Jamie breathlessly trotted back with his beloved football, she flashed Roman a warning glance and dropped into a crouch. 'That knee looks sore.'

'I didn't cry.'

'Well, I would have,' Marisa retorted.

'You're a girl.'

'Boys cry too.'

Her son looked doubtful. 'Do you cry?' he asked Roman.

She held her breath, fully anticipating a tough male macho response, only to release it when he replied.

'Everyone cries.'

'Come on, let's get that knee sorted and have some cake,' she said.

CHAPTER SIX

ROMAN WAS STANDING by the window when the door was flung open and Jamie bounced into the room displaying a boundless energy that made it hard to imagine him as a child who had had a life-threatening illness, his knee sporting a sticking plaster and his hands now clean.

Marisa followed close behind carrying a tray, which she set carefully down on the table between the two big comfy sofas, then she took a place on one and motioned Roman to sit opposite her.

He considered ignoring the invitation and sitting beside her but practicality won out over perversity. Even across the room the scent of her perfume—or was it just the scent of her skin?—brought back too many distracting memories, and hunger clawed in his belly.

'Do you want a biscuit, Jamie?'

'Can I have two?'

'No.' The child responded with a small shrug and grinned. 'Tea?' Her eyes brushed Roman's face.

He would have much preferred brandy but he nodded, unable to take his eyes off the little boy who was busy cramming his biscuit in his mouth. The son he had imagined in his head had been a blank canvas but he was discovering the reality was very different. Jamie was already a personality.

'Are you my mum's boyfriend?'

Roman's eyes flew wide as the four-year-old did what few others ever had—threw him totally.

Marisa choked on her first sip of tea. 'Jamie, you can't say something like that!'

'Why?' The child's mystification was genuine.

'Indeed, why?' There was nothing genuine about the puzzled look on Roman's face, but the taunting gleam in his eyes spoke volumes as he glanced at a pink-faced Marisa.

As the child exchanged a look with his father, oblivious to his identity, Marisa was suddenly struck by the striking similarity in their body language. Her throat aching, she jerked her eyes downwards, feeling something she didn't want to feel as she swallowed against the ache in her chest.

'Sam at nursery, his mum has a boyfriend and Libby Smith says her mummy has two, but I don't believe her. She shows off and she fibs. She says she can swim but I know she can't.'

'Can you swim?' Roman asked curiously.

'Y...' His eyes slid to his mother's face. 'Well, I can with arm bands on and I can kick harder than anything. Can I have another biscuit now, please?' His hand hovered over the plate. 'Chocolate?'

Marisa responded to the opportunistic request with a distracted, 'Yes.' Glad of the distraction as her son snatched one before she changed her mind, she watched him pull a toy car out of his pocket before he bounded across the room making the appropriate noises.

'You can be my mum's boyfriend if you like.'

Marisa could feel Roman's eyes on her face, but she refused to return his gaze, knowing full well she'd see mockery there and maybe something else... Besides, she would only end up staring at his mouth again and thinking about it sliding across her lips... The self-admission came with a tidal wave of heat that rose through her body until every inch of her skin tingled with embarrassment.

Or was that excitement?

'I'd prefer Ashley, but Mummy is too old for him.'

'Yes, she is much too old for him,' Roman agreed gravely.

'How old are you?'

'Thirty-one,' said Roman, feeling a lot older as he listened to the flow of childish confidences.

'I'm five next time, and I can already count to ten in French and I know *two* people who went to heaven. How many do you know?'

'Jamie, there are some bricks under the chair. Please will you go and put them back in the box?' Marisa instructed.

Roman, reeling and pale under his tan, directed his question in a low choked voice to Marisa. 'Does he mean...?'

Marisa, understanding shining in her eyes, tipped her head in confirmation, causing the cold knot in his belly to harden to an iron fist.

Shock bypassed his normal close-mouthed caution when it came to revealing anything about himself. 'And I thought *my* child-hood was traumatic!' Caught up in his own thoughts, Roman didn't register the expression on Marisa's face. 'He sounds so casual about knowing people who have died.' He found that almost as disturbing as the brutal facts themselves.

'Children who have been through what Jamie has, they grow up quickly in some ways, but they are remarkably resilient. More so sometimes than the adults.'

She spoke quietly, her soft voice carrying virtually no inflection but he could see the shadows in her eyes. For the first time he let himself think about what the nightmare experience must have felt like, wondering if her child was going to die. She had faced more than he had done in his life, and he felt humbled by the strength she had shown.

'Jamie knew how ill he was?' he asked.

'They don't lie to the children.'

'Even when the truth is—' He shook his head, appalled. 'I cannot imagine how hard it must have been for both of you.'

He had known his child literally for five minutes and already he was positive that if it were required he would lay down his life to spare him a moment's suffering. The absolute shock of this fresh discovery widened his eyes.

She would have done the same, he realised as he watched her throw out a word of encouragement and a smile to the child who was adding a final brick to the lopsided creation that looked in imminent danger of toppling.

But it hadn't been an option for her; instead, she'd had to sit there, day in and day out, watching her child suffering and feeling totally helpless. *Dios*, he could not even imagine the sheer horror of what she and Jamie had been through.

'I'm sorry.' The words emerged almost against his will, the deepening furrow in his broad brow an instinctive response to the inadequacy of the words he had never expected to hear himself voice.

She was desperate—wasn't that what Rio had said? Not that Roman had been listening, because he'd had no space in his head right then for reasons or excuses. Just anger, resentment and a strong sense of betrayal that still hadn't gone away, but he could see past it now, although he didn't want to, and it made him mad as hell to acknowledge even in the privacy of his own mind that Rio had only spoken the simple facts; Marisa had been desperate but not desperate enough to come to *him*.

And maybe she had been right?

He paused that chain of thought before it could get too uncomfortable, her soft voice providing the escape route that he grabbed hold of.

'It wasn't your fault that Jamie was ill.'

Her generosity was genuine enough to send a slug of shame through him. 'I should have been there for both of you.'

She had bent over to scoop up a couple of the stray toy building blocks from under a table, and as she straightened, her ponytail landed with a gentle thud between her narrow shoulder blades.

Face gently flushed from the exertion, she flashed a glance to the corner of the room where Jamie was now playing with his toy car again, before responding to his statement.

'You didn't know. I should have told you, I see that now, but at the time I was—' She turned her head but not before he had seen the sheen of unshed tears bright in her eyes.

Rio's words came back to him again. *Desperate.* She had been *desperate.*

Clearing her throat, she turned back to face him. 'When you're in a situation like that, the only people who actually understand, *really* understand, are those who are living through it too. They become in some ways your support network. You're all living in a bubble, and, although the world carries on as normal, for you nothing is normal even though you try your—' She stopped, a self-conscious expression seeping across her face as their eyes connected and she gave a tiny jerky motion of her head, looking confused, as though she'd never actually articulated those feelings before.

'So do you keep in touch with the other parents?'

'A few.' Her eyes filled with tears again and he saw her try to rapidly blink them away.

Roman considered himself immune to female tears and the soul-baring and accusations they frequently preceded. He generally pretended not to notice them and made himself scarce; he certainly never had to fight an urge to hold someone and tell them it was going to be all right. Even Marisa's prosaic sniff before she launched into husky speech again located an unexpected vulnerable spot inside him, awaking a tenderness he didn't know he possessed.

'Amy, she...' She glanced towards Jamie and Roman noticed with a touch of amused pride that his son had appropriated yet another biscuit while they'd been distracted in conversation. 'We were both single parents; everyone else was part of a couple.' She saw him flinch. 'I wasn't trying to...you know...make you feel guilty.'

'I know you weren't.' It was becoming more than clear to him that Marisa did not play the blame game.

'Actually I think Amy and I were lucky.' Marisa saw his eyes narrowed with scepticism and she hastily explained.

'From what I saw an ill child often puts a relationship under a lot of strain. At least two couples I met while Jamie was being treated are in the middle of a bitter divorce now and another couple are giving it another go, so who knows?'

'Maybe the cracks were already there in those relationships,' he suggested, threading his long fingers together as he looked at where Jamie had crawled under a table and was happily building a tower out of bricks. 'Or maybe most marriages, once you look beneath the surface, are pretty toxic.'

The cynicism in his voice drew a wince from Marisa—he really didn't seem to have a high view of marriage, which begged the question why had he once proposed to her?

'Why—' She stopped and pushed away the question that felt as though it belonged in another life now; the person she had been then no longer existed, the things she had felt, *longed* for, all gone, like smoke on the wind. She had completely changed so maybe he had changed too. Maybe he was sitting there congratulating himself on his own lucky escape from marrying her.

It turned out it wasn't his own escape he had been thinking of.

'My mother only started living again when she escaped her marriage.' Distracted for a moment from the shocking developments that were dominating his own personal life, it was almost relief for Roman to turn his inner anger and frustration to another situation that he had even less control over.

His mother had freed herself from her marriage to a man who wanted to control every aspect of her life, a man whose warped idea of love was to cut the object of his affections off from everyone else who cared for her, who was jealous of anyone who took her attention away from him—including his sons.

And here she was getting involved with a man with one failed marriage already behind him. The thought of the theatre director his mother had been with for the last two years etched a frown into his brow.

He didn't give a damn that the man was twelve years younger than her; he didn't care that he was successful enough not to be after her money. His mother was a happy, confident woman now but Roman couldn't get rid of the image of her as the woman she'd been before, afraid to make any decision for herself, while seeming happy and content to the outside world.

What if history repeated itself with this other man and Roman couldn't see past the happiness and contentment so he couldn't protect her just as he hadn't been able to protect her as a child?

'Why did you ask me to marry you?' Marisa asked, sounding as though she simply had to know.

His gaze slowly moved to her face.

'Do you expect me to say I was in love with you?'

He had thought it back then, but he wasn't about to admit to her something that even now he struggled to admit to himself.

His lip curled in self-contempt as he remembered thinking he had finally found his soulmate and the idea of losing her, of not spending every possible minute of the rest of his life with her, had seemed like an insanity.

She had had him at a golden glance, and he had run with reckless haste to claim the very thing he had spent his life avoiding, with consequences that only proved how right he had always been to avoid it.

'No, I…'

'Love can, I have heard tell, survive the cruel light of day. But what we shared was not love, it was likely just a…temporary insanity brought about by our seething hormones.

We wanted to get naked a lot, so it's perfectly understandable.'

Why it should hurt so much to hear him reduce what they had shared to a basic animal lust, Marisa didn't know, but it did.

'People get married all the time when they know they shouldn't... How many people have you heard say, "I wish I'd never married you"?'

'We didn't get married,' she said quietly.

'Then you could call us lucky.'

A whoop of delight as Jamie's tower toppled, scattering bricks across the wooden floor, broke the spell of Roman's brooding stare, and she smiled at her little boy.

'He seems to take some delight in destruction,' Roman commented with amusement.

'Yes, he is your average little boy, but so kind, as well. Last week his nursery visited a petting zoo and he was so gentle with the chicks and...' She stopped, her reminiscent smile fading as she felt a self-conscious flush run up under her skin. 'Sorry.'

'What for?'

'I can get a bit boring when I talk about Jamie.'

'Mothers are meant to think their children are perfect and I am not bored.'

'Does your mother know about—' She glanced at Jamie.

Roman shook his head. 'I haven't told her.' He supposed it was possible that Rio had told her as his twin seemed to have been taking a lot onto himself of late. 'I'll wait until she's out of hospital again.' Always supposing the damned boyfriend ever left her side, he brooded, thinking of the tender hand-holding scene he had walked in on when he'd last seen her.

'She must have been glad to see you,' Marisa said.

'Not so that you'd notice,' he admitted, his lips twitching into a wry smile as he recalled her exasperated, *I do not need a guard dog, Roman.*

He saw Marisa's startled expression and tacked on, 'She is not the world's best patient, because she isn't—*patient*, that is. And you can't really blame her as this thing has dragged on long enough already. She had the initial surgery in Switzerland after a skiing accident, where she broke her leg.'

Marisa winced at the explanation.

'It was a bad break. They pinned it, but there was a problem with the pin, so she's needed further surgery.'

Marisa made a soft sound of sympathy before her features suddenly froze in an expression of dawning surprise. 'Jamie has a grandmother.'

'Jamie has a father too,' he countered grimly.

Marisa sighed. She was getting tired of ducking the guilt and she really hadn't seen that one coming.

'I'll tell her about us when she is discharged.'

Marisa's chin went up. 'There is no us,' she said and immediately wished she hadn't; it sounded so petty and she knew he hadn't meant that sort of us.

'We are connected through Jamie whether you like it or not—and on that subject, I have a proposition.'

Marisa lowered her eyes, hearing the word *proposition* and remembering his proposal. She took a deep breath and cleared her mind and her expression. 'Well, let's hear it, then.'

'Beyond me being his father, Jamie has a

Spanish heritage that he knows nothing about and he should have access to that heritage.'

'Jamie is British.'

'He can be both; he can have two parents. He *has* two parents.'

Marisa sat there tensely waiting, wondering where this was going.

'I would like him to come to Spain.' She immediately recoiled and he tacked on sardonically, 'I am not about to snatch him from you—obviously you will come too.'

'Obviously,' she said coolly, not willing to own up to her moment of panic. 'Look, I can't just drop everything.' Her lips tightened at his assumption that she could rearrange her life at a moment's notice for his convenience. 'I have a very busy schedule, and I think it would be far better if you visited him here to begin with. I don't think that's unreasonable. You could take him out or—' She was running out of alternative suggestions when he cut across her.

'You do realise that this situation won't stay just between us for long?'

She looked at him blankly and shook her head as if she didn't understand what he meant, but she did—she just didn't want to think about it.

'It will not stay a secret, Marisa. My face and name are well known, and if I walk down the street with a child who looks like me—'

She shook her head, holding up her hand to silence him and thought, *Too much detail!* It was too late, though, her imagination was already conjuring up the tabloid headlines, and the effect of those on her own and, more importantly, Jamie's life.

'All right, I get it, but is it actually so inevitable? If we—'

'It's inevitable,' he bit back, scorn edging his softly spoken words. 'Unless you want me to visit my son under the cover of darkness?'

His sarcasm sailed over her head as dread congealed in an icy cold lump inside her stomach.

'Of course not!' she exclaimed.

'It will be easier if we manage the story ourselves.'

The words brought her eyes back to his face, to see that his eyes were narrowed in concentration. He sounded as if he were discussing a hostile takeover rather than their son...

Her eyes widened. *Their* son, she registered, shaken to her core. It was only one word but it represented a massive mental shift in her way of thinking, a shift that she had not been conscious of.

'*Manage!*' she echoed. 'How do you manage something like this?'

'We control the flow of information,' he explained, sounding a lot more boardroom than bestselling author. It made her wonder if he'd ever go back to work at the family company, and what had happened that had made him change direction so drastically.

'Which will be difficult if we are outed by some enterprising paparazzo with a long lens or a passer-by with a phone snaps me wheeling a pushchair.'

'He's four and a half. His push chair is an absolute last resort. He hates it.'

He arched a brow. 'I think you know what I'm saying, but it's true I know zero about children and even less about being a father, so it's just as well I have you to guide me, isn't it?'

'There's no need to be sarcastic,' she said, in no mood for some sort of conversational ping-pong match. 'There is no parenting handbook.

It's more an on-the-job learning experience. I'm still learning too.' Her eyes brushed the figure of their child engrossed in his game. 'And making mistakes,' she finished wearily.

She fought against the sense of helplessness she felt tightening its grip. The picture he painted of their immediate future was not one that gave her a lot to look forward to.

Roman frowned as she lifted a hand to her head, but as if she felt his scrutiny her eyes lifted. As their glances met the pulse of sexual tension that connected them seemed to flare like a streak of flame.

Marisa broke the connection and sat back in her seat, avoiding his eyes as she picked up a china teacup and lifted it to her lips, not seeming to notice it was empty.

'So this managing of the flow of information,' she said in a flat little voice. 'Do you have anything specific in mind or are you still working out the details?'

'I have something very specific in mind.'

Her enquiring golden gaze fluttered to his face.

'Well, I think it would be perfect if we had access to somewhere which is totally secure, where privacy is guaranteed and there are no prying eyes, like say a Spanish estate?'

'Or a prison?' she suggested bitterly, not hiding her displeasure at being played.

Something flashed across his face. 'I have heard it called that before, but there are no locks.'

'So much for security,' she muttered darkly.

His lips twitched appreciatively. 'I did not mean it literally. Look, why don't we call it a holiday? Let me get to know my son away from prying eyes, allow me to introduce him to his roots. We all need to know where we come from.'

She looked at him, the internal conflict she was fighting shining in her amber eyes.

'I think under the circumstances you owe me that much,' he said, with no qualms about pressing home an advantage when he sensed it looming on the horizon.

Her slender shoulders drooped as if she were carrying something too heavy to bear, and he watched as she ran the tip of her tongue across her dry lips. 'Three weeks.'

'I'll take that.' His eyes narrowed and it was clear to Marisa that he'd gone up a mental gear. He had already moved on, his sharp mind turning to the next sequence of events.

'I'll arrange the flight and let you know the details. I have a few things I need to sort out, but if you could be ready for around...ten a.m. tomorrow, I'll send a car—'

'No.'

His eyes landed on her face with an almost physical sensation. She smiled back with determined serenity and was rewarded by his frustrated frown.

'Don't bother with the car. I'll make my own way there and let you know what flight we get and when we land. If someone could get us from the airport that would be good.'

'*Someone?*'

She watched his features rearrange themselves, moving in a cycle that took mere seconds from astonishment to clenched-jawed annoyance, finally settling into cynical amusement.

The latter bothered Marisa the most and brought her chin up to a defiant, some might have suggested childish, angle.

'Are you sure about this, Marisa? You could

land at a private airport, with no crowds, queues, delays…?'

It was her turn to channel superior amusement as he dangled that carrot in front of her nose. 'Sounds lovely but I prefer not to be tied down to someone else's schedule.'

He tipped his head in acknowledgment and slowly, elegantly unfolded his long frame from the sofa. 'Jamie is a good flier, then?'

Anxious to reduce the extra height advantage he held over her, she sprang to her feet, dusting invisible specks from her sleeve as she dodged his gaze. 'Excellent,' she said smoothly, thinking wryly that there was a fifty-fifty chance she was right.

Their eyes moved in unison to the area where Jamie was playing, only to discover he was now curled up in a ball, thumb in his mouth, fast asleep.

'I've only ever seen a puppy do that,' Roman whispered.

'You don't have to whisper. He won't wake up.' She moved across the room and, despite her assurance, lowered her own voice as she posed over her shoulder, 'Do you mind seeing yourself out? I'll just take him to his room.'

She missed the flicker of expression on his face as he watched her scoop up the sleeping child into her arms with a smoothness that spoke of practice, the slender back she presented to him as much as her actions effectively shutting him out.

He slanted a last look at them before he turned and moved silently towards the door, struggling to combat a feeling that was utterly alien to him. It was such a weird reversal; he had spent his life avoiding women who were needy and now he found himself in a moment of weakness wanting a woman, a stiff-necked woman full of stubborn pride, to need him.

His hand was on the handle when a soft voice halted him.

He turned around, his breath catching in his throat. She was oblivious, he knew, to the image she presented standing there, the sleeping child cradled tightly against her body, his head tucked on her shoulder. Her face-framing silvery hair blazed with the sunshine that shone in through the window, and his hungry gaze roamed across her delicate features that didn't need anything cosmetic added to enhance their delicate cut-crystal beauty.

The sheer loveliness of her tentative smile hit him like a kick in the belly, releasing a flood of hot longing that he couldn't suppress.

For a long moment they stood there staring at one another, unspoken emotions zinging between them, until Roman found himself speaking, the words falling from his lips involuntarily, coming as much of a surprise to him as they seemed to be to her.

'I have a son.' He stared at Jamie's flushed sleeping face before shifting back to Marisa's. 'I cannot say yet if I will be a good father, but perhaps the best any of us can do is simply hope we do no harm.'

'You know, Roman, if I thought for *one micro moment* that you would be bad for Jamie,' she told him fiercely, 'in any way whatsoever, I would fight you tooth and nail to keep you out of his life.'

As her flashing amber eyes locked on his Roman felt a spark of unwilling admiration.

'So you don't think I would be bad for him?' He wished that he shared her confidence. He found himself fervently hoping that his son had inherited his mother's generosity of spirit.

'The jury is still out at the moment.' Her

beautiful smile took the sting out of the warning and the defensive stiffness from his spine. 'Don't overthink it; just love him—that should be enough.'

If only he shared her belief in the power of love, but Roman knew all about its destructive power. His father's love for his mother had definitely not been enough; it had been far too much!

'I will send a car.'

Still wondering if she had imagined the shadow moving across his face, Marisa gave a sigh. Did he think if she conceded on one point she was ready to devolve all her decisions to him?

'I already said that I prefer to make my own way to Spain.' She stood still, hugging Jamie's warm body to her, enduring the forensic searching scrutiny of Roman's dark stare.

'Are you trying to make a point?'

'No, I'm just not comfortable being organised.'

He lifted his hands in an acquiescent gesture and took a step back. 'Fair enough.'

CHAPTER SEVEN

HOW MANY TIMES had he visited the Bardales family estate in Spain since he and Rio had inherited it from their father? Three or four occasions and on only one of those had he extended his stay overnight. This might have explained the shock displayed by the staff on his unexpected arrival. Even the undemonstrative estate manager who had walked in as Roman was giving instructions concerning the guests they were to expect had looked shaken. In fact, the other man had been so thrown by Roman's presence that his handshake had turned into an affectionate bear hug for the man he had known since he was a boy.

He wasn't the only member of staff to seem pleased to see him, but Roman felt it wasn't an affection he deserved considering how long he had avoided the place that came burdened with too many memories.

Roman rarely slept late, but he had finally

fallen asleep around five a.m. and by the time he clawed his way out of his restless slumber he glanced at his phone, saw the time and groaned.

He fell out of bed and into the car, the heavy traffic he had to negotiate on his way to the airport not improving the tension that had climbed into his shoulders. He was reluctant to admit even to himself that he was nervous, but this was definitely not your average day at the office. Even clinging to a rock face by a fingertip above a drop of several thousand feet would have been infinitely more relaxing.

He wasn't late, but he wasn't early either, and his efforts to check out the situation were frustrated by the arrivals board, which seemed to have gone totally blank.

He was making his way through the crowded concourse to the information desk when an overheard snippet of conversation made him stop. He tapped the man who had been speaking on his shoulder.

'London plane? You said they had lost contact with the London plane?'

The man nodded. 'You have someone on it?'

'My family.' Roman felt as if an icy fist had

reached into his chest and grasped his heart. Then he shook his head, stubbornly refusing to accept that they could have…

'Which flight are they on…the one from Heathrow or Gatwick?'

Roman just stared at him blankly. His brain had stopped working and the suffocating black coldness was pressing in on him.

'Here you are. I've been looking for you everywhere!'

Roman spun around. Marisa was standing there looking tired, cranky and quite incredibly beautiful as she expertly jiggled a pushchair in which Jamie lay fast asleep.

She didn't have a clue what was about to happen as he reached out for her, one hand curving around the nape of her neck the other one framing her face. Her eyes flew wide in comprehension a second before his mouth came down hard on hers in a long plundering, sensually explosive kiss that went on and on.

When it ended she was leaning into him, her knees shaking as she gasped for breath. He set her back on her feet a little way away from him.

Jamie, she saw, had not stirred.

'Why on earth did you do that?' She struggled to inject righteous indignation into her voice but she didn't quite get there, probably because she couldn't stop looking at his mouth, remembering that glorious kiss.

She had wanted it to go on for ever.

Roman dug his hands into his pockets. 'A London flight has lost radio contact with air traffic control and I thought you were on it.' Just one simple sentence and yet it covered a whole range of emotions that he had never felt before, and never wanted to feel ever again.

'Oh...so...*that* was why—'

'I was just glad to see you were alive.'

'Right, well... OK, then.'

In an action that had all the hallmarks of compulsion he was unable to control, he extended his hand back towards her face.

As Marisa's voice had earlier, her chain of thought broke, dilated pupils eating up the gold of her eyes. The quiver deep inside her expanded as he extended his reach, his square-tipped fingers brushing a stray strand of silvery-blonde hair from her cheek, the pad of his thumb trailing along the angle of her delicate jaw while he performed his task.

It was almost nothing, a whisper touch, but the nothing had the breath leaving her parted lips in a sharp sibilant hiss. The tenderness of his unexpected action made her throat tighten and she felt the heat of unshed tears stinging the backs of her eyelids.

Obeying an instinct too strong to resist, she turned her face until her cheek was nestled into his cupped palm and she was vaguely conscious of a foreign-sounding expletive too soft for her to catch.

Jamie's sleepy murmur brought her to her senses and, appalled by her weakness but with her skin still being bombarded with needle-sharp prickles of attraction, she laid a soothing protective hand on her son's head.

'Last resort?'

She looked up and nodded to the hand luggage balanced on the handles of the pushchair. 'I couldn't manage everything.' She paused and took a deep breath. 'I really wish I'd come with you now.'

'Yes, you should have.' Those few awful minutes when he'd thought he might have lost them for ever had taken several years off his life. 'Let me take it.'

'Thanks.' Their eyes locked and she immediately looked away.

The pushchair was easier to manoeuvre without the hand luggage, so she was able to keep up with his long-legged stride until she felt obliged to breathlessly point out the signs for the luggage collection they had just walked past.

'That's all been taken care of. This way.' He glanced down at a now wide-awake Jamie and winked, and the smaller version of his own eyes widened and, after a pause, delivered a blink back. Then a small hand came up and covered one eye before he blinked again as they passed under an archway that took them out of sight of the cameras and into a brightly lit underground parking area.

Marisa took in the empty parking spaces with reserved signs on them, the occupied ones filled with an assortment of top-of-the-range vehicles, which explained the visible security presence and numerous CCTV cameras.

A man in uniform wearing a headset acknowledged them with a tip of his head as they walked past.

'Can I have a biscuit?' came a small voice.

'How long have you been awake?' Marisa exclaimed. She'd been nervous of Jamie's reaction if he woke in a strange place and found Roman there too but he seemed remarkably relaxed, looking around with interest.

'I wasn't asleep.' He gave her a cheeky grin from his pushchair and added, 'I was just resting my eyes.'

Marisa laughed, the soft musical sound bouncing off the low ceiling and walls.

Listening to the interchange, Roman found himself feeling like an intruder; they had a relationship that he was not part of.

Was he really envying the thing that he had spent his whole adult life avoiding?

He heard Marisa say, 'Say hello to Roman, sweetie…'

Roman dropped into a crouch beside the pushchair but, instead of responding to his own hello, Jamie reached out and touched Roman's cheek, startling an expression from him that made Marisa look away. 'Are you growing a beard?'

'Not deliberately.'

Marisa could hear the smile in his voice and a deep quiver shimmered through her body as from the forbidden depths of her brain a memory surfaced. They had been lying amid a tumble of sheets, their sweat-soaked bodies cooling, her nostrils quivering as she'd inhaled the warm, musky male scent of his body.

Her chest had lifted in a sigh as she'd lain there experiencing a cell-deep contentment that had been entirely new to her. In some ways, the aftermath of sex had felt even more intimate to her than the act itself.

'I need a shave,' he'd murmured.

Her eyes had opened at the touch of his fingers on her breast. Despite the aftershocks of the climax still rippling through her body she'd felt her insides tighten as she'd watched his fingers massaging the sensitised, still-tingling pink skin of her breast.

He'd stopped then, self-reproach in his face, and had lifted a hand to his face, drawing it down across the abrasive dark growth on his jaw.

She'd put her hand over his, drawing her own

fingers down the stubble. *'I like it,'* she'd whispered.

'I will have a beard when I grow to be a man and I'll be tall too.'

Her son's confident pronouncement dragged Marisa back to the present with a disorientating abruptness. She felt a tide of guilty colour wash over her skin and she struggled to share the amusement with Roman as they exchanged glances above their son's head.

'That sounds like a plan,' Roman said.

Marisa was glad for the distraction when Jamie demanded her attention then. 'So can I?'

'Can you what?'

'Have two biscuits?'

'Later,' Marisa said, before adopting a diversionary tactic. 'Which car do you think is Roman's?'

'The one with our cases and the policeman standing by it.'

Her son, it turned out, was more observant than she was. The car in question was a big four-wheel drive with blacked-out windows standing about fifty feet away, and there was a security guard, not a policeman, standing beside the luggage she had last seen in London.

'I want to walk,' Jamie said, pulling at his safety harness.

Roman glanced at Marisa, who nodded before he carefully unfastened the strap and put the wriggling child on his feet.

'I want my case.'

'Fine, but you must hold my hand because of the traffic.'

Jamie's childish features settled into a mulish expression she knew all too well as he tucked his hand behind his back. 'But there isn't any—'

Before Marisa could respond Roman stepped forward. 'I need some help to put the cases in the car,' he said casually.

Jamie looked at the hand extended to him for a moment before his mulish expression became a sunny smile. 'OK...' He glanced at his mother. 'Can I?'

'Off you go.'

Watching them walk away hand in hand, Marisa experienced a rush of emotions at the poignant picture of father and son. She felt recede some of the doubts she'd struggled with over her decision to make this trip. It was an effort to hold her emotions back as she followed them, very conscious of the ache in her chest. For someone who'd said he had no experience of children, Roman was doing a pretty good job.

CHAPTER EIGHT

THE FOUR-WHEEL DRIVE they were eventually installed in was roomy, and the 'nice smell' that Jamie mentioned, ensconced in a booster seat in the back, was that of soft leather and newness.

It was not the only thing that Jamie commented on as they left the city lights behind them. He seemed to be enjoying a second wind, although finally the flow of questions petered out and his head began to droop once again.

Roman turned up the air conditioning on his side of the car, and a welcome blast of fresh air removed some of the distracting scent of Marisa's perfume from his nostrils.

After silence had reigned for five minutes Roman risked a quiet question.

'Is he asleep?'

He felt Marisa glance his way and saw her head nod in the periphery of his vision.

'So he's a good traveller?'

'Not always,' Marisa replied honestly, hoping that Jamie's best-behaviour mode hadn't raised false expectations in Roman. He was being a model child, so far only asking once if they were there yet, and happily accepting Roman's response that he would tell him when they were.

Jamie hadn't even requested a toilet break and the chocolate biscuit she had finally allowed him—because sometimes it was just not worth the fight—had gone mostly in his mouth.

At least when he was awake she had been able to focus on him and the distractions his multitude of questions had afforded.

Now he was asleep, looking cute in his booster seat, cuddling the dog-eared giraffe that had been his companion and comfort all through his illness, and she was left with no option but to make polite conversation with Roman, polite conversation that did not involve mentioning that searing kiss at the airport.

She just wished she could stop thinking about it.

Roman's gaze kept repeatedly flashing to the reflection of his sleeping son in the rear-view mirror.

'Does he always ask so many questions?' He was here to ask the questions, and Marisa—his glance flickered to her profile—was here to drive him to distraction.

The kiss had not been a good thing. It had just made him realise what he was missing and had provided even more fuel for the ever-present ache inside him.

'Yes, but he doesn't always sleep like this, but it was his first flight and he bounced the entire way, he was so excited. Oh, is this—'

She strained her neck to look out of the window and Roman knew what she'd be seeing. They were passing through a massive ornate wrought-iron gate. The gatehouse beside it was lit up but although there wasn't anyone in it, there were security cameras mounted there. The road they were now driving along had fewer ruts for Roman to negotiate and it was less winding than the one they'd been on previously.

'Yes, we're on the estate now,' he confirmed, his thoughts travelling back to that moment in the airport when he'd thought the very worst had happened. Maybe you had to face having something snatched away before you realised how much you wanted it?

With the gut-freezing fear had come clarity. In that moment the idea of being a distant but supportive figure in his son's life, never realistic, had become a complete non-starter. Marisa had asked him what he wanted and he had dodged the issue because he hadn't known then. He had still been in denial and avoiding owning the fact that being a father absolutely terrified him.

Now he had shrugged off the uncertainty, he knew the answer he would give her. He wanted to be a father to Jamie, the best father he could be. He might not be very good, but if he messed up, no, he amended with a flash of uncharacteristic humility, *when* he messed up, as he no doubt would, he was sure that Marisa would put him right. His glance slid sideways long enough to register the delicacy of her profile as she gazed out of the window.

Long enough to disintegrate his determination to not want her as his body clenched in hungry desire. It was a complication that he would need to deal with at some point soon but his ability to effortlessly multitask appeared to have deserted him.

He thought of the glazed passion burning in her eyes after he had kissed her at the airport. Stopping so abruptly had just about killed him, so maybe he'd just let nature take its course?

Aware that his thoughts had taken a dangerous direction, he blocked them, but not before he realised that despite all the danger he had courted, all the extreme sports he had thrown himself into, this was the most alive he had felt in over five years.

His expression one of fake ferocious concentration, he turned his attention back to the road that he knew like the back of his hand from the days when he had learnt to drive in the gardener's Jeep. Until Rio, taking his turn in the driver's seat, had swerved to avoid a wild boar and they'd ended up upside down in a ditch. Roman had an interesting scar to show for it and Rio had climbed out without a scratch.

His father had banned them from driving after that, and grounded them for a month, but the real punishment had been his sacking of the gardener whose car they had totalled, making sure that his sons knew the man's fate was on their heads.

That ex-gardener was now his mother's personal driver but at the time it had felt like something they would never recover from.

How his mind took the seemingly seamless leap from the man who was now his mother's personal driver to the burning question of whether he and Marisa could live under the same roof and not end up sharing a bed would remain for ever one of life's mysteries, but it was there now, in his head, and it showed remarkable staying power.

'Are you all right?' Marisa sat on her own hands while her eyes kept straying to his. Roman's long brown fingers curled around the steering wheel were exerting a strange fascination for her, but it turned to concern when his light grip tightened until his knuckles turned an almost bloodless white.

He shot her a frowning look. 'I'd be better if you stopped asking stupid questions.'

As she hadn't said a word for a good five minutes the implication that she had been bombarding him with chit-chat struck her as

deeply unfair. Lips twisted, she debated with
herself whether to challenge him, but decided
against it as she conceded, at least in the privacy of her own head, that he was allowed to
be irritated after being forced to drive so far to
collect them. Also she didn't want to distract
him as the road they were travelling along had
some pretty scary hairpin bends and a few
dramatic drops.

It was ten minutes later, and Marisa had
maintained her silence, if you discounted the
couple of gasps when a bend had revealed a
particularly awesome vista. She was starting
to get an idea of the scale of the estate when
they hit an avenue of tall trees lining what she
assumed must be the last part of the drive.
They were up-lit by spaced floodlights that
gave the impression they were driving through
a tunnel of light. As they crested a hill to see
the *castillo* come into view Marisa caught her
breath. The same floodlit effect gave the aged
stone walls of the imposing façade a silvered
tinge, while the lights shining out from the
windows glowed a warm gold that matched
the last fading rays of a magnificent sunset.

Marisa had not been anticipating anything

on this scale. She was accustomed to a home that many considered grand, but this building eclipsed anything she had seen.

It was a castle in every sense of the word.

A possibility that ought to have occurred to her on the journey here now popped into her head, and she wondered if there would be family members on hand to judge her.

This had all happened so quickly, the pace that everything had moved at was a million miles from her normal controlled, cautious approach where there were normally no surprises, unpleasant or otherwise.

She slid a covert glance at Roman's patrician profile, the carved angles emphasised by the reflection from the outside lighting. It was hard to think of life around Roman as not containing surprises—admittedly not quite the sort that her dad had used to spring on her. She really couldn't imagine Roman announcing that it would be fun to sell his Rolls-Royce so they could travel on public transport—but it was another reason she told herself to be glad that this visit was not a prequel to spending her whole life with him. She wasn't interested in living a life of surprises any more.

This was about what was best for Jamie, who had a right to know his father so long as that father was good for him.

Transferring her gaze to the façade of the looming building that looked grander and more ancient the nearer they got, she was conscious of the heavy nervous thud of her heartbeat. The darkness didn't help—it probably exaggerated the imposing vibe. Not that she was holding out much hope of it appearing any more cosy in daylight, but she would settle for less daunting.

She was starting to realise that there were a lot of other questions she ought to have been asking instead of simply allowing Roman to call the shots and rush her.

'Will any of your family be here?' It wasn't as if there wasn't room—a dozen families could have shared the place and not bumped into one another.

He turned his head briefly, his expression impossible to read in the fading light, his proud profile a dark silhouette. 'Unlikely. I assume my brother will be avoiding me for the considerable future.'

She took the sardonic comment as a reminder that she was responsible for a falling-out between the twins and squirmed uneasily in her soft leather seat, but then a noise from the back seat made her turn her head to look at her son.

Jamie was still sleeping, one hand thrown above his head, his face flushed. When he had been ill she had only ever thought a day ahead, and the only thing she had dreamt of was him being well. It had certainly never crossed her mind that she was in some way depriving him because he was an only child. She had been an only child and she hadn't felt deprived, but last week when she had picked him up for a play date and seen him watching on as his little friend dropped a sloppy kiss on his chubby baby sister's forehead it had made her wonder.

Jamie's expression had brought a lump to her throat, despite the fact the children's mother had admitted ruefully that for the first six months big brother had been jealous of his new sister.

She hadn't missed out as a child, but *twins*, she thought, had a particularly special bond that shouldn't be broken. She settled back into her seat, silently vowing that if there was some way she could repair the damage she'd wrought, she would, though at that moment, reading Roman's grim profile, she couldn't summon much optimism on the subject of her influence over him. He was probably still thinking about the last few hours that he'd never have back again.

Looking at him was a mistake, because once she'd started it was hard to stop. There was something about his features that just pulled her in... Her eyelids half closed as her thoughts drifted back to the airport again, to the moment when his fingers had cupped her cheek. The gesture connected in her mind to the ache she felt deep inside.

Confusion pressed down on her; she had never needed a male shoulder to lean on. Sure, Rupert had been there for her in her hour of need, but his condition had meant that for most of their relationship he had been the one doing the leaning and that had felt normal to her. Her dad had been like a kid pretending to be an adult sometimes, and from early on it had been up to her to look out for him.

She comforted herself with the knowledge that the airport situation had been the result

of a combination of factors—all high stress—
and it didn't mean she had turned needy. She
dragged her gaze free from his face, turning
a deaf ear to the voice in her head that pointed
out the multitude of flaws in her argument.

As the car crunched over the gravel, the
purr of the powerful engine that had been
imperceptible became more noticeable by its
absence as they drew to a halt. The sudden silence made her aware of every sound inside
the intimate space of the interior, the soft hiss
of their intermingled breathing, the squeak of
fabric on leather and, more distant, the eerie
sound of an owl's call as Roman opened his
door, allowing the fresh night air to flood the
car.

She turned her questioning gaze to him and
found her eyes snared yet again. Something
in his steady unblinking stare and the impression the air was being sucked out of the space
around her left her breathless, making her rush
into speech. She said the first thing that came
into her head, wincing slightly that the tone
was all wrong; her voice sounded too breathless, too desperate.

'I can't imagine looking at someone and seeing the face I look at every day in the mirror.'

She watched one dark brow lift before the motion-detection lights on the gravel-covered forecourt that had illuminated the interior of the car chose to go out, adding another layer of darkness to the enclosed space.

It wasn't just the lines of his face that the darkness blurred, it blurred her resolve and it lowered her resistance…*to what, exactly?* she asked herself.

She shivered. She didn't really want to know the answer. It was bad enough she was unable to pretend that it was Roman she was fighting. The battle was with herself and the forbidden emotions, the *hunger* he awoke inside her.

She gave her head a tiny shake as if to dislodge the thought. She didn't want to think about it; she *wouldn't*.

She tensed as his deep gravelly textured voice broke the silence. 'We might look alike, but we are very different people.'

Marisa tore her eyes from his shadowed face, too spooked by the fascination it held for her to ponder the odd inflection in his flat statement.

She turned back and found that Roman was looking at her, making no attempt to leave the car. Her stomach muscles quivered with a combination of fear and something she refused to identify as excitement as she resisted the pull of the invisible silken thread that in her imagination joined them.

'How so different?' she asked, though she thought she already knew part of the answer. She had looked at his brother and her nerve endings had not tingled, there had been no silent thread connecting them and she had not wanted to breathe in the scent of Rio. She brought her thoughts to an abrupt halt, realising to her horror that she had begun to lean in towards Roman.

'From Rio?' he said, sounding as though he had forgotten what he had been talking about.

'Yes.' She straightened up in her seat, pushing her hair behind her ears as the outside lights, perhaps activated by some night creature, clicked on again.

'People say I am more like my father than Rio.' The bleak comment was delivered with a twist of his lips.

She felt pinned to her seat like a suicidal

moth drawn to a flame by his dark complex stare.

'Is that a bad thing?' she wondered huskily.

The question seemed to jolt him, leaving Marisa with the impression that he regretted saying anything at all. She felt a surge of frustration; she had met clams that revealed more about themselves than him. *Or maybe that's just with me*, she mused. *Maybe he shares his innermost thoughts with other people...other women...?*

Unbidden, an image of the blonde with the impressive chest that he'd been glued to during the rash of publicity shots for one of his films a few years ago flashed into her mind. Maybe that woman brought out a different side to Roman? Maybe he showed his vulnerable side to her...?

She pushed the thought away, dodging the accusing voice in her head that was yelling, *You're jealous!* The idea was simply ridiculous. The last thing she wanted was to know what made Roman tick. The man was too intense for words, and just breathing the same air as him gave her a headache. As for him having a vulnerable side, it would be her first mistake to imagine he even had one.

No, Marisa, your first mistake was to walk into that hotel over five years ago.

A furrow formed between his sable brows. 'What's wrong?' he barked.

She shrugged at the accusing question. 'What do you mean? Why should anything be wrong?'

'You squeaked.'

Her chin went up. 'I did not—' she began and then broke off. This, she decided, could get very childish very quickly. 'I have a headache.' To her relief he appeared to accept the half-lie, as actually she did have the beginning of a headache. 'It's been a long day.' She glanced up at the building and thought, *It doesn't look like it'll be getting better any time soon.* 'I still think it would have been simpler if you'd got to know Jamie at home.'

One dark brow elevated. 'So you were inviting me to be your guest?'

'God, no!' The words were out before she could stop them. 'I mean—'

'Yes?' he pressed when she halted, looking interested in her answer.

She compressed her lips and flung him an angry look. She was too tired for a conversational battle of attrition. 'You could have picked him up, gone for trips—' *And I could have observed from a safe distance, and there would have been no kisses.*

'Trips?'

'He likes the zoo.' He didn't seem too impressed by her hasty improvisation.

'So your expert advice is that a few day trips to the zoo is the best way to get to know my son? That it would make up for the last four and a half years.'

'He happens to like the zoo,' she gritted back.

'So you said.'

'I hadn't given much thought to alternatives because you were so obviously not going to accept the idea.' No, he'd wanted everything to be all on his terms, and because she felt so guilty she had agreed to it all in a moment of weakness. He'd claimed she owed him and he was right.

'Look, I'm aware that this isn't ideal.' His eyes flickered to the shadow of his ancestral home. 'It's not exactly warm and intimate, I know,' he admitted. 'But it is away from prying eyes.'

Marisa lowered her gaze, musing ruefully that could only be a good thing. Even thinking of the words *warm* and *intimate* in connection with Roman was dangerous.

'Don't you have somewhere else that is less—'

'I keep hotel suites in a few city locations,' Roman said, anticipating a surprised if not disapproving reaction to a lifestyle choice that had not won universal approval.

What was to his mind a practical option, his mother saw as some sort of inability to put down roots. Everyone, she claimed, needed a home. When he pointed out that he owned a tropical beach house and a mountain cabin, she pointed out that, no matter how picturesque it was, a place without road access and a half-day trek to reach it, or one that involved stilts and was only accessible by boat, could only be called homes by someone who was running away.

She didn't specify from what, and she was, as he had told her, over-exaggerating the situation. His choice not to buy a more traditional property was a purely practical solution. Why buy somewhere that would be empty most of the year when you could keep luxury suites where all your needs were catered for in several cities without the bother of maintenance or staff?

'You live in hotels?'

He'd encountered reactions to his lifestyle before, but not like the sympathy he saw in her face.

'It gets a bit boring, doesn't it?'

'You have lived in *hotels*?'

Marisa nodded. 'I've lived in lots of different places. My dad travelled and I travelled with him. There was one time when he had his credit card refused at the—' She caught sight of Roman's concerned expression and stopped. 'Sometimes we travelled first class and sometimes... Well, Dad was always generous even when he had no money and he had friends who were equally generous with their sofas and floors.'

'That must have been...worrying for you.'

'Not for him.' He'd always said he didn't need to worry because she did it for him. 'He always saw the bright side of life.'

'And you?'

'I didn't mind not having money sometimes. The posh hotels were nice but the novelty of on-tap room service and every whim catered for fades.' Instead, she had longed for the familiarity of a room and belongings that were all her own. 'It must have been fun for you and your brother growing up here.' Unaware of the wistful envy in her voice, she imagined two boys having a ball exploring a place that likely as not boasted secret rooms and, on first appearances, dungeons.

'It had its moments.'

A rather cryptic non-answer, she thought.

The information he'd offered about his parents' marriage and the heavy hints that his relationship with his father had not been very healthy would explain the conflicting emotions she saw on his face before his mask slid back into place.

'I think a home is people, not a place,' she mused half to herself. Jamie was her home and she was his.

'Are you offering to be my home? A roof over my head, my harbour in a storm...?'

His pointed sarcasm brought a flush to her

cheeks and an unexpected knife thrust of pain to the region where her heart lived. 'No, of course not. I just meant—' A flustered hand pressed to her chest as though she expected to see blood seeping through her fingers and she stopped babbling; she had no idea what she meant.

The sardonic glitter faded from his eyes. 'I don't like to stay in one place for too long.'

Was he talking about a place or people? she wondered. Had the hinted-at bad memories from his childhood prevented him from putting down roots? Or was his comment shorthand for his preference for one-night stands and temporary affairs? Just the idea added nausea to her physical symptoms.

'We could not be more different, then,' she said quietly. 'But then I'm a mother and a child needs stability, routine—' She stopped, realising she'd started out talking about Jamie but what she actually meant was herself. They were the things that she craved.

'I'm a father,' he cut in harshly.

Unable to react to his brusque interruption or protest his interpretation of her comment, because he had virtually thrown himself out of the car door in his haste to get away from her, she opened the passenger door. Exiting the car with less fluid grace than Roman, she turned and found herself thigh to thigh, shoulder to shoulder with him.

She took an involuntary step backwards and mumbled, 'S-sorry,' to his chest. She would have taken a second distancing step back but with no warning his hand shot out, his fingers curling around her upper arm.

Heart pounding, her face lifted slowly to his, and she heard the breath snag in his throat as desire and longing twisted and expanded inside her chest.

Trapped as much by the desire coursing in a hot stream through her body as the hypnotic pull of his obsidian stare, she stood there quivering—*aching*. She had never reacted to any man this way, any man but Roman. He seemed to have direct access to a part of her that scared her.

A part of her that didn't recognise common sense or self-preservation, a part of her that didn't care about consequences.

The combination of passion and fear reflected in the golden pools of her eyes should have made Roman step back but he found himself stepping closer instead, pushing his body into hers as his hand slid to the small of her back, pulling her against him until their bodies were sealed hip to hip.

He saw the moment she felt the carnal imprint of his erection, her pupils dilated and he heard the throaty little gasp that left her parted lips.

He could feel a growl in his throat as he bent his head lower towards her plump, trembling lips, his blood heating as he thought of plunging his tongue past them and tasting the moist warmth of her mouth.

'Oh, my God, what was that?'

Startled, he dropped his hand from her waist as she turned around, her wide fearful eyes scanning the darkness above their heads where moments before a ghostly apparition, a flash of white, and the beating of wings had disturbed the silence.

'An owl hunting.'

A predator, Marisa thought, looking straight at another predator, all six feet four inches of him standing there, his chest heaving as he dragged air into his lungs like a drowning man.

What am I doing?

'I thought it was a ghost.'

'There are no ghosts here. The past is dead and gone and it would be a mistake to try to resurrect it.'

Well, that didn't sound as if he was talking about nocturnal birdlife, but it did sound as if he was talking about their almost kiss. She was grateful the half-light hid her shamed blush.

She got the message loud and clear. Once he had wanted more than she was able to give, now it seemed that all he wanted from her was sex—and then only on his terms.

'I'm not trying to resurrect anything. I just want to get Jamie indoors and settled for the night,' she explained quietly. 'So what are we waiting for—the reception committee?'

'Don't worry, there won't be anyone around at this hour.'

He had reasoned that it would be less stressful for a child to arrive at a new place if there weren't lots of new people to cope with, as well, though he had to admit Jamie seemed a remarkably resilient child.

The swell of pride that tightened his chest as he turned to look at his sleeping son took him by surprise.

'So how do we do this?' Finding it hard to be the person asking for instructions, he directed his question to Marisa, aware as he looked at her of a fresh flare in the hunger that was still thrumming through his body. He'd told her he didn't want to resurrect the past, but that was because he had enough to deal with in the present without going around opening old wounds. He just hoped the logic would filter down at some point to his rampant hormones.

The things this woman did to him remained stronger than anything he had ever experienced; nothing had changed over the years they'd spent apart, and that was the problem. There was no volume control on the hunger she aroused in him; there was no halfway house. It was full on, and *it* controlled *him*.

He shouldn't have to remind himself that acting on it was a bad idea considering what had happened the last time.

Circumstances had brought her back into his life but Roman had moved on. Marisa was still his weakness but he told himself he had strengthened his defences. He lifted his avid gaze from the cushiony softness of her lips and swallowed.

'Will he wake up if we move him?' he asked huskily.

'That's really doubtful. He's flat out.' Despite her claim, as she scooped Jamie up, she closed her car door quietly and saw that Roman was following suit. As her eyes brushed his she hastily stepped back to put some distance between them, in the process backing into a low hedge. Immediately the warm night air was filled with the heavy summery scent of lavender.

'This way.' He gestured for her to walk ahead of him and tried not to notice the lush tautness of her bottom and the gorgeous length of her slim legs.

CHAPTER NINE

THOUGH THE PREDICTABLY massive space of the hallway was empty it was flooded with light. Marisa blinked and looked around with genuine pleasure.

The heavy dark wood panelling and stone walls could have been oppressive but somehow they weren't. The darkness was alleviated by the brilliant glowing threads of the antique rugs underfoot and the series of framed photographic landscapes on the walls.

'Did your mother plan the decor?'

'My mother hasn't been here since the divorce.' His lips quirked into a fleeting ironic half-smile as he added, 'As I said, other than a staff of thirty or so we will have our privacy.'

She couldn't return his smile; privacy of any sort was the last thing she needed. What she needed was space.

So why are you just standing there?

The question could have just as easily been

directed at Roman, who continued to stare at her over Jamie's curly head.

'It's a lot to take in,' she said quietly.

'I'll show you to your rooms.'

He led her up the curved stone staircase to the galleried landing above.

'There a small salon just down there.' He nodded to the right-hand side of a long corridor with an ornately stuccoed barrelled ceiling. 'Your rooms are this way.' He took a right turn, this corridor a twin of the other.

'Here they are.' The door opened into a sitting room, but she didn't waste much time looking around as Jamie had woken up and started crying.

Correctly assessing her priorities, he pointed her to an open door. 'His bedroom is through there at the end.'

It took her hardly any time at all to settle Jamie, who'd fallen straight back to sleep before she had even pulled down the covers on his bed.

Checking the baby monitor, which was standing on a low table in the room, was working, she explored the other rooms in this guest suite before she returned to the sitting room.

She paused in the doorway. Roman was standing with his shoulder wedged against the wall, staring out of the stone mullioned window. He levered himself away and half turned.

'Did he go back to sleep?'

Lingering in the doorway, fighting a reluctance to enter, she nodded. *You're acting as if he's about to leap on you*, mocked the voice in her head.

It was the mortifying possibility she might be the one to do the leaping that continued to hold her back.

'He was so exhausted he barely stirred at all, not even when I put him in his pyjamas. He's totally out.'

'I asked for some supper to be left for us.'

It wasn't the idea of sitting in some dauntingly enormous room at a table laden with candelabra and antique crystal that made her stomach flip, it was the knowledge of the person who would inevitably be sitting opposite her, which was ridiculous. It was something she was going to have to learn to cope with—but not today, she decided, pushing this hill to climb into the future with a mental sigh as the almost-kiss outside by the car still weighed guiltily on her conscience.

'That's thoughtful.' Marisa, who had been hiding behind the heavy strands of hair that had escaped the knot on her nape, pushed them back before carefully closing the baby gate between the nursery and the sitting room, but left the door ajar. She'd been pleased to see there was a similar arrangement between the anteroom with the useful compact little kitchen, which connected to her own bedroom, and the nursery, so at night she could leave the doors ajar.

'But I'm not really hungry.' Her stomach chose that moment to growl so loudly to reveal her lie that his lips twitched.

Her lips stretched into a rueful smile that reached her amber eyes and immediately lit up her face, dissolving some of the tension.

'All right, I am starving actually,' she admitted, pressing a hand to her stomach. 'But I'll be fine.' There seemed to be plenty of tea and coffee in the kitchen area. 'I really don't want Jamie to wake up alone in a strange place.' This place was so enormous that even if she was alerted by the baby intercom it would take her far too long to reach him.

'I assumed you wouldn't,' he replied calmly. 'I'll bring up a tray for you.'

'*You* will?'

Her astonishment seemed to amuse him. 'On occasion I have been known to tie my own shoelaces. Make yourself comfortable and I'll be back shortly.' The advice was slung over his shoulder as he exited through the door.

What she would *really* have liked was to take advantage of that spectacular en suite bathroom with its copper tub massive enough that you could swim or at least float in it. It was really calling to her and she could almost hear it as she lifted a lid on first one and then another of the glass flagons. Each sweet-smelling oil had an even more gorgeously heady scent than the one before it.

She reached out and experimentally pressed a button set into the marble tiled wall, jumping when the room was filled with music. Hastily depressing it again, she stood statue-still, listening intently, her eyes wide above the hand pressed to her mouth, but after a minute she relaxed; the noise had not woken Jamie.

Resisting the bath, she stripped off her clothes and left them where they fell, suddenly too weary to care about the crumpled heap.

The fabric of the building might be ancient but it was clear that it boasted the latest technology. She ran a finger around the edge of the bath tub and allowed herself an indulgent moment to fantasise wistfully about floating in the foamy sweet-smelling suds, just to wash away the day's grime and ease the ache of tension in her limbs, before regretfully turning her back on it.

Grabbing a towel from the pile that was neatly stacked on a chest, she headed for the shower, very conscious that she had no idea how long she had before Roman appeared with her food, and as she didn't want to be drifting around in a towel when he did she allowed herself the minimum time under the reviving spray.

Still damp and swathed in a towel, her skin pink and tingling from the arrows of water, she tipped out her carefully packed overnight bag onto the silk cover of the four-poster bed. Rifling through the spilled contents, she extracted the clean underclothes and the jeans and tee shirt she always packed in her hand luggage after the last time her hold cases had ended up on another continent, leaving her without even a toothbrush.

At least this time her luggage was not too far away, just in the car outside, but in some ways it was equally inaccessible. She had no intention of risking getting lost or setting off some sort of alarm trying to find it.

She had the basics, but not the time; in a feverish haste she had reached the stage of dragging a comb through her hair when she heard a sound which, unless she was being visited by one of the resident ghosts the place probably boasted, was Roman.

It offended her innately neat nature but she ignored the accusing pile of clothes she could see through the open bathroom door and glanced in the mirror, wishing she had time to disguise the violet smudges beneath her eyes, before she dashed for the door, arriving in the sitting room breathless and barefoot. The latter didn't register with her until his interest in her pink-painted toenails brought her own attention downwards.

At least it was an excuse not to look at him

and it gave her heart a chance to slow to a bearable canter.

'I was in a hurry,' she said, her voice indistinct as she shook her wet head, sending drops of moisture flying, and wondering why on earth she sounded so defensive.

Roman wrenched his eyes clear of her denim-covered thighs, trying hard not to notice that she possessed the sort of legs that seemed to go on for ever. Her black tee shirt was emblazoned with a daisy logo and was tucked neatly into her narrow waist.

Catching the direction of his gaze and misinterpreting it, she touched the daisy with a not quite steady finger. 'Jamie was shopping with me and he loved this one. I'm afraid the rest of my bags are still in the car.'

'He has excellent taste.' Roman nodded towards the door. 'The rest of your things are there. I'll take them through into your room.'

Her eyes flew to the stack of cases by the door that led out to the corridor, then back to his face. 'How?'

'I waved my magic...' He paused, because she didn't look in the mood to appreciate his laboured humour. 'I brought them up for you before I collected the supper tray.'

He had been in her room, just a wall separating him from her naked in the shower... She gulped. 'I didn't hear you come in.'

'Relax, I left them outside the door until I came back. I waited to be invited in.'

She felt her stomach muscles tremble in response to the predatory gleam in his dark eyes. 'Just like a vampire.' It didn't seem such a bad analogy at all; weren't vampires these days all sexy as hell and equally dangerous?

'Except with no blood involved.' Just a hell of a lot of self-control. What Roman hadn't said was that he had opened the door, heard the shower and closed it again, because he didn't trust himself not to go to her.

She reacted to the comment with a weak smile flashing out before she worked up the courage to meet his disconcertingly intense stare.

Dios, she looked as if stubbornness was the only thing keeping her upright. 'Sit down,' he said, his abrupt delivery hiding his concern.

His lip curled in self-disgust as she walked towards one of the sofas. He'd been too busy noticing how great her lush body looked in jeans to notice until now the cell-deep weariness in her body language.

She looked as though it was an effort to lift up her feet as she walked across to the sofa.

'You're tired.'

Her head lifted at the accusation.

'When did you last sleep?'

'What is this, twenty questions?'

Arms folded across his chest, he stood there waiting for her answer, and finally Marisa gave a sigh of defeat. 'All right,' she fired back. 'I'm tired but I've had a lot on my mind. Just don't fuss.' She knew from experience that even when you felt you couldn't go on for another minute—and there had been more days like that than she wanted to recall when Jamie had been ill—there were always reserves to call on.

The water-darkened ends of her hair brushed her neck as she sat down before carefully tucking the offending strands behind her ears.

'I have not exactly dressed for dinner,' he said abruptly as he bent forward to lay down the tray he was carrying on the coffee table between the two sofas.

She tucked her legs under her, thinking that he didn't need to dress for anything; he looked gorgeous whatever he was wearing—or not wearing. She veiled her gaze guiltily as the thought slipped past her tired defences. After a few hours' sleep this situation was going to be so much easier to cope with.

Want to bet?

'I'm not really hungry.'

He rolled his eyes. 'Not that again. You will eat,' he remarked pleasantly. 'Or I will feed you myself,' he promised with a steely smile that left his eyes grimly determined.

She snorted to show how unimpressed she was but, despite her claim, she felt her empty stomach rumble once more when he whipped off the dome cover with a magician's flourish to reveal a plate containing a selection of de-licious-looking, artfully arranged sandwiches.

'I'd say I made them with my own fair hands but I didn't. The tea and coffee are, however, all my own work.' He nodded to the pots he had balanced either end of the tray as, instead of taking a seat on the other sofa or, and this was the preferred option for Marisa, heading for the door, he sat down beside her.

Marisa directed her gaze at the safer option, another plate, this one containing beautifully decorated small cakes that would have graced the window of any high-class patisserie.

Not looking at him didn't make her any less skin-tinglingly conscious of his closeness.

'Eat!'

Eyes slitted, she slung him a recalcitrant look, but reached for a sandwich. One bite of the layers of smoked salmon and cream cheese sandwiched between moist rye bread and she forgot her reluctance.

She sampled two more before sitting back with her arms folded. 'Well,' she challenged. 'Do I pass?'

He gave a concessionary grunt.

'So what happens now? Oh, not now as in we go to bed—' He snorted as an expression of comical horror spread across her face while she issued a hot-faced correction. 'That is go to bed, but not together— I mean—'

'I know what you mean and the answer is it's up to you what happens next. I'm assuming that Jamie might be tired tomorrow and a little off his game after the journey?'

'Cranky as hell probably. I usually try to keep to his routine as much as possible.'

'And his routine is?'

'When he is not in nursery I allow him to watch one of his cartoons after breakfast.' She supposed that wasn't an option here. 'Ash or I usually take him for a walk later.' Turning over a piece of rotting wood on the ground and discovering all the creeping life beneath could keep Jamie fascinated for hours. She found herself suddenly wondering what Roman had been like as a child. Had he approached life with curiosity and enthusiasm as Jamie did? Then she stopped wondering because the price was an ache in her chest. 'In the afternoon it depends.'

'He mentioned enjoying swimming. We have an indoor pool and a gym complex.'

'Of course you do,' she muttered, trying to ignore the arm he had thrown across the back of the sofa.

'The outdoor pool is heated if you think that would be better for him.'

'Doesn't it seem a waste to you? Having all this here and no one to enjoy it?' Aside from the invisible staff of dozens, which she would no doubt encounter tomorrow.

'Rio and I never expected to inherit it.' His eyes flashed her way before he turned back to the contemplation of his threaded fingers. 'Disinheriting us from this place was always his threat of first resort and we both assumed he'd gone through with it, but he ended up leaving us the lot. I think he expected us to fail, but then he had never made any attempt to include us, or teach us anything about his empire. He was a total bastard, but at least he was a bastard with a golden touch. It wouldn't have mattered a jot to him that our failure would have a knock-on effect that would deprive so many families of their livelihoods too.'

'He sounds like—' Words failed her as indignation for Roman and his twin swelled in her chest, well, mostly for Roman, if she was honest. It was beyond her comprehension that a parent could harm their child like that, toying with their emotions.

'If you're into labels, he ticked all the boxes of a narcissist, a malignant narcissist.' He offered up the information in a curiously emotionless voice. 'He was an expert at manipulation. He became incredibly vindictive whenever he felt threatened by literally any decision my mother made without him. He took it as a personal affront and he responded by belittling her, and undermining her confidence until she was utterly dependent on him. His jealousy was totally toxic—'

'Coercive control,' she said, remembering an article she had read about the subject.

His dark brows lifted. 'I believe that is the term, yes.'

'But your mother escaped.'

'Yes, she escaped love, but she is a remarkably strong woman and not everyone would have been so lucky.'

Did he even realise what he had said? she wondered. Did he know how revealing his choice of words was? For Roman love was clearly something you escaped from, a trap. That seemed very sad to her, as did the suspicion that her own deception had probably played some part in setting this view of his in concrete.

As she struggled against a fresh wave of guilt she became belatedly aware that while he spoke she had turned towards him until she now faced him, her legs still tucked underneath her, the arm she placed along the back of the sofa stretched out so that her position mirrored his, their fingertips almost touching.

As surreptitiously as she could manage she slowly retracted her arm at the same time as she unfolded her legs and placed her bare feet on the floor, and she swivelled around so that she sat shoulder to shoulder against him.

'A pity that there is no DNA test for being a bad father. Some men should not have children.'

His pronouncement had a hard uncompromising note in it that made her twist back towards him. His earlier comments about being more like his father than his brother floated to the surface in her memory and she realised that he was really talking about himself, that it was Roman's inner fear that he would hurt those he loved as his father had.

A hundred images flashed through her mind before she accepted the truth—he *did* love Jamie. He might be the most aggravating, stubborn, difficult man she had ever met but Roman was no monster.

'You are *nothing* like the man you have described to me.' She caught the flash of some emotion in his face as their eyes connected and consciously lowered the tone of her voice before she added carefully, but firmly, 'If you were I wouldn't be here. I've already told you that if I thought you being around Jamie would harm him, I would build a fifty-foot-high wall to keep you out.

'I was close to my father,' she volunteered, not aware that her own expression softened as she spoke. 'But there were only the two of us.'

'Your mother died?'

'My mother walked out on us soon after I was born,' she revealed with a casualness that to Roman's watchful eyes seemed too contrived. As if she still carried the invisible scars of the rejection but would die before she'd show it. 'She didn't like being a mother because she felt it "crushed her vitality".'

He didn't need to see quotation marks painted in the air to know she was directly quoting her mother. They were words that should have had a crushing impact, but her expression was serene. True, there was a sadness in her smile, but there was no discernible resentment that he could detect.

He thought about the extensive file headed 'Marisa Rayner' that remained unopened on his laptop.

Why commission something and not make use of it? He had fully intended to but in the short intervening time between requesting an in-depth report on Marisa's life and it dropping into his email inbox something had changed.

He had been reluctant to admit it. He'd told himself that he was too busy to read it, that he wasn't in the right frame of mind to view it objectively, he was too angry or too tired… But his inventive powers had eventually deserted him and he was left with only the truth, which was that he still wanted to know all about her, but he wanted her to volunteer the information.

'She actually said that to you?'

'Gracious, no…' She flashed him a small smile, and in the semi-light her eyes made him think of pools of liquid gold.

'Well, I suppose she *might* have,' Marisa conceded, oblivious to his discomfort. 'But as I was two months old the last time we met in person, I don't really recall.'

Did the joking response hide a multitude of

hurt, he wondered, or was she *really* as all right with being rejected as she sounded?

'Actually she wrote me a letter when she left, for me to read when Dad thought I was old enough.' It wasn't the letter that had hurt, it was what she had discovered when she'd wanted to find out more about her mother, when her seventeen-year-old self had wondered if perhaps they could be friends as adults.

When she had found her mother online she had discovered that the woman who'd felt unable to be her mother was now remarried and was the mother to three step-children as well as a child of her own, Marisa's half-sister.

No, they could never be friends.

She levelled her clear gaze on Roman's face and thought about the demons he would never reveal, let alone allow her near enough to help him move past. And she *wanted* to help him, she *wanted*... Shock filtered into her eyes as she stilled, and everything inside her seemed to stop as the truth hit her.

She loved Roman; she had when he'd proposed to her, but she had taken refuge from the truth, telling herself it was just physical because the reality was too painful to own—

the fact that she'd had to walk away from the only man she had ever loved.

The man who would never forgive her for her double deception of being married and hiding the existence of his child from him. If he had ever loved her, she had surely killed that love stone dead years ago, and that was her punishment to bear.

'Are you all right?'

'Fine,' she lied, forcing a smile. 'I loved my father. And he loved me, but he left me in a desperate situation when he died. Without Rupert I really don't know what would have happened to me. But that's the way with addicts and Dad was a reckless gambler who walked the line between being legal and being a con man, although mostly he stayed on the right side of the law. He never really grew up, my mother deserted her own child, but nevertheless I am not like either of them. Who you are isn't all about DNA and you can't allow an accident of birth to define who you are.'

Roman closed his eyes, wishing he had her certainty and hoping that she never had that belief crushed, because he knew what that felt like. 'You really believe that, don't you?'

She nodded. 'Yes,' she said simply. 'I do.'
She eased her back away from the sofa. 'Do
you mind if I go to bed now? I'm pretty tired.'

He vaulted to his feet without a word. 'I'll
see you tomorrow. I hope Jamie has an undis-
turbed night.' He turned away but then swung
back almost immediately. 'I'd say whistle if
you need anything but in this place I wouldn't
hear you.' He picked up her mobile phone from
where it lay on the coffee table and, flicking
through it, he punched in a rapid series of num-
bers. 'So call me if there are any problems.'

'How did you know my phone pin?'

'Jamie's date of birth? You really should double protect.'

Outside the door he leaned against the wall
and wished that protection against the hunger Marisa aroused in him were so readily
available.

CHAPTER TEN

MARISA WAS IN her bedroom hanging her belongings in the cavernous walk-in wardrobe
when she heard the knock. Tightening the belt
on her robe, she hurried past Jamie, who was
still in his pyjamas, bent over colouring books
and crayons he had spread across the coffee
table.

She took a deep breath and opened the door.
Despite the mood-lowering sense of anticli-
max when she saw a young woman in a neat
uniform standing there, she kept her smile
painted in place.

'*Buenos dias, señora.*'

'*Buenos dias.*'

'I am just asking if you would like to take
your breakfast here or in the breakfast room
with Señor Roman.'

'I'm hungry, Mum!'

'All right, big ears,' she tossed back. 'In here,
if that is no problem.'

'And what would *señora* like?'

'Coffee, juice and toast, please. Oh, and some fruit would be lovely too.'

'Scrambled egg,' came Jamie's voice.

Marisa smiled at the girl. 'And scrambled egg.'

'*Sí, señora.*' She bobbed a little curtsy and walked away swiftly.

'Have you cleaned your teeth yet?'

'Yes,' he said with his hand over his mouth.

Marisa's lips twitched. 'Go clean them again, please. I can see you found the clothes I left on your bed but you did actually wash your face, didn't you?'

Jamie looked hurt. 'Of course I did.'

Squatting down to readjust the top that Jamie had put on back to front, she let it pass, putting a hand on the floor to stop herself losing her balance when there was a knock on the door. She had already opened the doors to the balcony where the table and chairs afforded a gorgeous view of the acres of green manicured lawn and the mountains beyond.

'Come in!' she yelled, then as the door opened she asked without turning around,

'Could you put it on the balcony, please? It's such a glorious morning.'

'Sí, señora.'

She almost lost her balance before finding her centre of gravity and rising rapidly to her feet. 'Roman!' Tall, effortlessly elegant and showing no after-effects from yesterday's emotional dramas, he made her heart pick up tempo. 'I thought you were the—'

'Maria.' His grin flashed, making her remember how easily he could charm her when he wanted to. 'An easy mistake to make. Many have commented on the likeness.'

Roman's lips twitched as she tightened the knot on her robe, but she couldn't add a few more inches to the length and it showed an amazing amount of her smooth shapely legs, which he thoroughly enjoyed looking at. He was able to observe her tousled, just-got-out-of-bed appearance without feeling tortured, because there was nothing to be tortured about. She was utterly gorgeous and he wanted her.

There were two options: he either did something about it or he didn't. Neither choice was going to have life-changing consequences. If he opted for the sex, he had no doubt it would be absolutely fantastic.

His sleepless night had not been a total waste. After ruminating for hours, he now knew he was seeing problems where there were just choices, and nothing, as he reminded himself again, was life-changing.

Jamie was life-changing, and now that he'd had the time to consider it objectively Roman realised that his son was not just life-changing, but life-enhancing.

Jamie's mother, on the other hand, well, that ship had sailed years ago. Roman had been a fool to propose to her, and, although at first she had taken a part of him with her that had left him feeling as though he had lost a limb, he had rebuilt his protective walls until they now formed an impenetrable barrier.

Even if he hadn't, it would take a very stupid man to allow a woman to do that to him twice, especially one who had already displayed a disturbing ability to wander around inside his head.

Marisa fought off a smile at his teasing and bit her quivering lip. 'Sure, you and Maria could be twins.' She sucked in a dismayed breath but the words were out before she could pull them back.

'I already have a twin. I believe you know him.'

And they were right back onto the subject that could never be a winner for her, but she squared her jaw. There were limits and she was getting tired of dissolving into an apologetic heap all the time. 'Not really. I've only ever seen him when he looks as if he is wrestling with a choice between the fire or the frying pan. I imagine he has his lighter moments.'

'Rio is considered in every way more upbeat than me. I am the deep thinker, apparently.' His grin did not reach his dark heavy-lidded eyes.

'Which is not saying very much.'

His sudden laugh dissolved the tension before it reached critical mass.

'So do you want this breakfast on the balcony?'

She nodded. 'Come along, Jamie.'

She ushered Jamie through the door to the balcony, following the tall figure who was positioning their breakfast on the wrought-iron table.

'I like it here,' Jamie declared.

'Do you, darling?'

'I'm glad he likes it. It'll be his one day or at least half of it will be. I imagine Rio's children will inherit the other half of the place.' Her eyes flew wide open and he laughed. 'You really haven't considered that, have you?'

Recovering from the shock, she rallied. 'Don't be stupid. I'm the woman who married a dying man for his money, ask anyone.' She heard the bitterness in her voice and winced. The scar on that particular wound was not as healed as she liked to think.

Forgetting that he had thought exactly that about her, he felt an urge to wipe the shadows from her face and berate the idiots who had put them there. 'Anyone that actually counts?'

Her burst of angry resentment fizzled away. 'Thanks for that. I know it's stupid to let it bother me but the story was doing the rounds when I first discovered I was pregnant and it was sort of a double whammy, though when it became public knowledge I was pregnant I morphed into a lonely brave widow overnight.'

She glanced towards Jamie, who was ignoring them and tucking into his breakfast, and she smiled. Seeing him wolf down food never failed to make her happy.

'He has a robust appetite.'

She nodded and said quietly, 'For so long he had no appetite at all and it seemed like he was fading away before my eyes.'

'You will, as well, if you don't eat. Anyway, I came to ask if you would like the guided tour in, say, an hour.'

'I would love to, but Jamie has been up since five.' At least it had given her the opportunity to finally enjoy the pleasures of the decadent bath.

'Which means you have been up since five too.'

She shrugged. 'Give it another hour and he'll be fading. He'll need a nap.'

She saw the disappointment on Roman's face and found herself suggesting, 'How about this afternoon instead?'

'That sounds like a good option but, in the meantime, how about I give the you the grown-up tour this morning? I'm sure we can cover more ground without Jamie.'

Marisa froze. She didn't want to be without Jamie. Jamie's presence was her shield, her protection against the feelings she didn't want Roman to pick up on, the ones she didn't want to feel.

If that made her a coward, she really didn't care.

'Sorry,' she said, adopting an unconvincing expression of regret as she leaned forward to snatch a piece of fruit off the breakfast tray. 'I couldn't possibly leave him.' She bit into a juicy peach and wiped the juice off her chin with a self-conscious grimace of apology.

'You could,' he said, while in his head he was tasting the sweetness of peach juice in her mouth and the resultant rise in his core temperature made him glad of the light breeze. 'Maria, who you've already met, would be more than happy to babysit. I'd say being the eldest of seven makes her more than qualified and I have personally witnessed her keep several feral brothers in line without breaking a sweat. She is truly a phenomenon.'

'She seems a bit wasted carrying trays, then.'

'She is off to train as a children's nurse next year.' He offered up the information smug in the knowledge that he had delivered a deal clincher. 'So...?'

'All right, I suppose so.' It wasn't exactly a gracious acceptance but he didn't seem to notice. After he had left she comforted herself with the fact that a tour couldn't take long, and she was making a fuss about nothing; it wasn't as if they were talking about a candlelit meal.

She was wrong; it did take a long, *very* long time.

The previous night she had not really taken on board the sheer vastness of the place or the number of people it seemed to employ. Aside from the private rooms, and the multiple banquet-size spaces and numerous bedroom suites, there were the domestic areas; not just the kitchen complex with its walk-in fridges and freezer and numerous ancillary rooms, but offices that housed the army of people involved in the running of several thousand acres of the estate, which boasted a bewildering diversity of industry from an organic vineyard to an area of productive forestry.

She would have been interested because Roman was a very well-informed guide, but he was still Roman and she had no Jamie to hide behind.

She had a suspicion that her fear, well founded, of revealing by a look, a gesture or a word the true depth of her feelings made her appear stiff, and her monosyllabic responses earned her more than a couple of puzzled looks.

But she could cope a lot better with his puzzled looks than with his pity—or he might even be angry? It was not a mystery she was in any hurry to solve, even though normally she relished a puzzle.

There was one thing that aroused her curiosity as they walked through the bewildering network of rooms and corridors. The staff they met, especially the ones that had known Roman as a child, displayed an obvious fondness for him, and Roman clearly felt the same, considering his relaxed manner with them.

There was respect and fondness on both sides and for someone who professed to hate this place he seemed to have a great deal of knowledge of its workings.

They had only explored a fraction of the buildings, she suspected, when he led her outside. The heat of the sun after the cool afforded by the thick stone walls hit her like a wall and she was grateful of the thin-strapped sundress she had chosen to wear. She was glad she had applied a liberal coating of suncream to her exposed flesh, but beside her Roman didn't appear to even notice the heat.

'You must need an army of gardeners.'

'Some, but they are not here today. There is a horticultural show on locally, so they have decamped en masse. The tennis courts are that way.'

She could make out some green through the screen of trees in the direction he pointed. She had left behind her idea that this would take half an hour tops when he mentioned visiting the olive groves that were only half a mile away, groves which apparently kept the estate supplied with their own olive oil all year-round.

She had rather tetchily pointed out that as no one lived here that couldn't be so difficult, at which point he had made her feel silly by explaining about all the families that lived on the estate as well as the satellite farms.

'Would you like to see the pool now?'

She dragged her eyes away from admiring his impossibly long eyelashes. 'No, that's fine. I'm sure you have other things to do. You've already been very kind with your time—' Her voice faded in the face of his unblinking stare.

'I am rarely kind, *mi vida*.' The slow, contemplative, wolflike smile that accompanied his drawled observation sent a shiver right down to her toes.

'I just meant—'

'This way…' He placed his hand between her shoulder blades, his eyes darkening as he felt the silky warmth of her suncreamed flesh.

His light touch carried an electrical charge that sent a convulsive shiver over which she had no control through Marisa's body, silencing the protest on the tip of her tongue.

'Are you cold?'

'No, I'm fine.' Shrugging off his touch would have been too revealing of her helpless reaction so she had no option but to endure the torture.

Her escape in the end didn't come in the form of a rehearsed ploy, but a natural spontaneous reaction to the sight of the huge outdoor pool.

Roman watched with a smile, contrasting her childlike enthusiasm with the image of serene elegance she projected in public. Right at that moment she looked just like a carefree teenager.

She balanced on the edge, taking it all in. It wasn't just the size; it was the way it was landscaped almost organically into its setting. Along one length was a series of arches housing stone benches and formal potted palms; the other length was landscaped with opulent-looking greenery interspersed with splashes of colour provided by exotic flowers. Beyond the waterfall that cascaded over artfully arranged rocks, there was a terracotta-roofed gazebo that sheltered low daybeds piled high with cushions.

This was one aspect of a billionaire lifestyle that she had no problems with! She kicked off her sandals and flexed her toes against the marble tiles swirled with pink that edged the pool. By contrast the pool itself looked as though it was scooped out of solid polished stone.

'Are those reeds?' she exclaimed, directing an enquiring look over her shoulder before she turned back to look at the greenery growing in the water.

'They provide a natural filter because there are no chemicals in the water.'

'I might camp here.' Her childish enthusiasm was contagious.

'You enjoy roughing it, then?'

She threw him a twinkling grin of reciprocal amusement that faded when she realised who she was with. This rapport would only ever be an illusion and there was far too much risk in lowering her guard around Roman.

'This is all pretty spectacular.'

Roman felt a sting of frustration as he sensed the restraint in her response, as if she was suddenly thinking twice about each syllable before she gave voice to an entire sentence.

Marisa blinked and closed her eyes as a sunbeam fractured on the water's surface, dazzling her.

There were some moments in life that were indelibly imprinted on your consciousness and this, he recognised, was one of them. He would never forget the image of Marisa, slim and supple, her body curved, poised like a dancer on the edge of the pool with her head thrown back, eyes closed, her face lifted to the sun.

'You look like a nymph. Is the water calling to you?'

She turned, shading her eyes before she turned back to the pool. 'I wish I'd thought to wear my swimsuit,' she admitted, gazing deep into the inviting turquoise depths.

He walked towards her. 'You really don't need one.'

She shook her head then as comprehension dawned, and darted him a shocked look.

'You know you want to,' he taunted, sliding a finger under the top button of his shirt.

'You wouldn't,' Marisa gasped with a weak laugh, but she knew of course that he would.

Another button and then another followed. 'You don't have to watch,' he taunted.

Actually she did, and she stood there, throat dry, one hand pressed to her parted lips, unable to tear her eyes off the slow teasing reveal as each successive button slipped from its mooring. His shirt gaped a little more, revealing another tantalising section of golden chest and ridged washboard-flat belly.

'Roman...you... Someone might see!' Her voice was barely more than an agonised husky whisper.

'Would that be so terrible?'

'Don't. I—' She took a step backwards, then another, then his own cry of warning blended in with the splash as she hit the water backwards. Her own scream was lost beneath the surface as she sank like a stone, hitting the bottom before she popped back up like a cork only moments later. She spluttered, choking a little as her head broke the surface.

Once he saw she was all right Roman started to laugh.

Treading water, half the pool streaming down her face, Marisa dragged back the tails of her saturated hair from her face and directed her wrathful incredulous gaze at the heartless figure standing there, immaculate and dry, and roaring his head off.

'You think this is f...funny,' she choked. 'You...you...' Her voice was suspended by another fit of coughing to the backing track of his laughter.

Recovering slightly, she hit at the surface of

the water, angrily pounding it with both hands, which only made him laugh louder when her feeble efforts failed to direct much more than a drop on his tailored linen trousers.

Teeth gritted in determination, she flipped onto her back and beat at the water with her feet until she sank.

When she surfaced again he was still standing there, as dry as a bone, his hands thrust deep inside his pockets. 'Sorry,' he said, not looking the least bit sorry.

Marisa smiled and floated forward, her arm barely raising a ripple now as she slid gracefully through the water. His own smile died as he watched her progress, completely riveted. She was as innately elegant in the water as she was on land.

Marisa reached the side of the pool and began to tread water. 'I suppose I must have looked pretty funny,' she commented, tilting back her head to look at the tall figure at the poolside. She stretched up a hand, pushing the sagging strap of her sundress that was floating around her like a bell up along the curve of her arm. 'Give me a hand up?'

The moment he reached down, long brown

fingers extended to catch her wrist to haul her out, she took a deep breath, and sank to the bottom, using her foot to spring-board up out of the water. As she broke the surface her hand shot out and as she grabbed his extended wrist, she fell back into the water, holding on hard.

Caught by surprise, he seemed to hover on the edge for what seemed like an age before he lost his balance, though somehow he still managed to twist so that he hit the water in a creditably clean dive and emerged only a few feet away.

'You little—'

She saw the retribution shining in his eyes. 'No, Roman!' she exclaimed, holding out a hand and shaking her head.

He shot her a white grin and she felt her pounding heart respond to his devilish teasing. 'Yes... I think yes...'

With a squeal she turned and began to swim away. Even hampered by her clothes her body was sleek in the water and she was fast but not fast enough, because he overtook her in seconds.

He caught her calf and sank with her; she went down twisting and turning like an otter to free herself, looking like a mermaid as she struggled to escape his grip, her hair floating like pale fronds of exotic seaweed around her face.

When they broke the surface he had her around the waist, her back against his front as he pulled her in close.

'Surrender?' he said in her ear.

She went limp in his arms. 'Yes.'

The moment his grip relaxed she slithered away and swam a few strokes before she flipped over and suspended her hands, patting the water either side to keep herself afloat and laughing her triumph at him.

Roman, the water streaming off his brown face, his dark hair slicked back, didn't return her smile, the sudden intensity of his stare making her own smile flatten, the sparkle in her eyes fading as, heart thudding with a mixture of excitement and fear, she waited for him to cover the distance between them in a couple of powerful strokes.

When he stopped and lifted his head he was only a foot away.

'Roman.' Her lips moved but she couldn't

hear her breathy whisper above the frantic
thud of her heart.

Their glances caught and held.

Unable to think beyond the need pounding inside her, she watched Roman reach out
to her, his fingers sliding over her wet hair
as he cupped his hand around the back of her
head.

There was no resistance in her as she floated
into him, her face coming up to his, her nose
grazing the side of his own. This no longer felt
like a game; it felt urgent, the urgency inside
her as strong as the need to draw in oxygen.

She didn't close her eyes even when his face
blurred darkly through her half-closed lids and
the hissing ebb and flow of their breaths mingled and became one.

Feeling the *rightness* of it, she tilted her head
fractionally to one side to allow him access.
He covered her mouth, her lips parting as the
tip of his tongue traced a path along the plump
lower curve before, with a groan, he plunged
his tongue inside her mouth.

With an answering groan, her legs wrapping
themselves around his waist to anchor herself

up tight against his body, she kissed him back, matching his frantic hunger with her own. She could feel the heat of his body even through the layers of wet clothes as she pressed close, but still not close enough as the hunger that had exploded inside her took control.

The kiss was so all-consuming that she wasn't really conscious that they had sunk beneath the water until her lungs began to scream and in unison they kicked for the surface. They floated apart dragging air into their lungs, until he had enough to strike out for the side of the pool. Beside him Marisa matched him measured stroke for measured stroke.

He hauled himself out of the pool in one smooth fluid motion, the ripple of the powerful muscles in his shoulders and back visible through the clinging fabric of his shirt.

She watched, waiting for the hand he stretched down, allowing him to pull her up as though she weighed nothing until she was standing beside him.

'Ro—' Her voice was lost in his mouth, the kiss fierce, and hungry.

She kissed him back without restraint, giving in to the craving that sang through her blood. Her arms were around his neck when he scooped her up and carried her to the gazebo and laid her down on the daybed, pushing some of the cushions to the floor to make space.

CHAPTER ELEVEN

SHE WAS OUT of the water but Marisa still felt as if she were floating as she lay there on the daybed, her heart pounding in heavy anticipation as she watched him begin to fight his way out of his saturated clothes.

His shirt fell first, and his damp skin gleamed gold in the sunlight. He was beautiful and she was mesmerised but, even so, there was still a tiny shred of sanity filtering into her overheated brain.

'Someone might see us...' she murmured, and felt a surge of relief when he ignored her and unzipped his trousers and tore himself loose. A moment later he was standing there naked, and the ache of longing inside was almost too much to bear. Every individual nerve ending was screaming, and a keening moan of need vibrated in her throat as she raised herself up on one elbow.

Eyes blazing, utterly wild, he fell down to his

knees beside the daybed, pushing aside more of the cushions to frame her face with his big hands. Marisa's hands were on his body as the force of his kiss bent her backwards onto the bed. Her fingers glided over the hard ridges of muscle in his powerful shoulders and back and then moved lower, down his flat belly, then even lower, causing him to suck in a sharp breath when she cupped his hard, hot length in her hand.

'So hot, so smooth—'

Roman swore, knowing he was perilously close to losing control. He pulled back, sitting on his heels as he took her hands from his body and raised them above her head.

The wet sundress came away easily and landed with a soggy thud on the floor feet away. His burning glance was almost hot enough to evaporate the water on her skin as it roamed over the slim, supple curves of her body.

'I think you'll be more comfortable without this,' he rasped, pulling down one of the thin straps that supported the tiny lacy bra she wore over one smooth shoulder.

She blinked and sighed. 'I will be more comfortable with you inside me.'

His polished ebony eyes flamed at the throaty provocation and his hands were trembling as he applied himself to removing the last physical impediments to satisfying her wish.

It took him what felt like a century to peel off the bra. Wet, it had adhered slickly like a second skin to her body, the now transparent fabric outlining the puckering skin of her areolae and the thrusting prominence of her erect nipples.

When he had finally exposed her body to his hungry gaze his frustration gave way to ruthless desire.

'You are so beautiful!' he groaned, lowering his length onto the narrow bed beside her and watching her face as the first skin-to-skin contact drew a low feral cry from deep inside her chest.

He rolled her under him and, resting on his elbows, kissed her almost savagely while he nudged her legs apart with his knees.

Marisa could feel the heat engulfing her

body, moist and waiting, when he slid into her in one slow, measured thrust.

A deep growl vibrated in his chest as she tightened around him, and he gritted his teeth, his blazing eyes devouring her flushed, aroused face as he began to move, increasing his speed and drawing a series of fractured cries of encouragement from her lips as the delicious pressure between them built.

When their climax came, for Marisa the release was so intense that she almost blacked out, the pleasure almost too sharp, too sweet, but she held on and slowly drifted back to earth, her head tucked into the angle of his jaw, her legs wrapped tightly around his waist.

As her sense of self slowly filtered back into her brain, the first strands of self-consciousness began to take control.

Suddenly feeling intensely vulnerable, she unwrapped her legs and rolled away to lie stiff and still by his side.

He had a forearm across his eyes and she had no idea what he was thinking. Then again, she told herself bitterly, why should he be thinking anything? It was only sex for him.

Roman felt her slide away from him with

a sense of regret. Her warmth gone, he felt the coldness seep back into him even though it was thirty degrees in the shade. He fought the irrational urge to drag her back against him and feel her burrow into him, as he lay there trying to insulate himself from the emotional fallout of what had just happened between them.

There didn't have to be any fallout; he had to accept it was just sex, great sex but just sex. He could deal with that; it was the unwanted emotions that complicated things.

He felt the cushions beneath him shift as she quietly got up. He opened his eyes ignoring the feeling of *rightness* that had stubbornly lingered, despite his best efforts to ignore it.

He propped himself up on one elbow in time to catch a glimpse of her narrow back and the tight peachy curve of her bottom, the gentle swell emphasising the length of her long coltish legs. He felt his sated body stir with desire that pooled heavy in his groin as he watched her drag the wet sundress over her head and a moment later her slim curves were enveloped in the loose folds of material.

She picked up the bra, which now had a little tear in it, and her panties, and squeezed out the excess moisture. Shoving them into one of the big pockets in the skirt of her dress, she looked around for her sandals.

'What are you doing?'

Her gaze lifted but her eyes skittered away from his, the veneer of calm thin enough to reveal the delicate quivering muscles along her jaw, the blue-veined pulse throbbing against the transparent skin of her temple.

'Exactly what it looks like. I need to get back to Jamie.'

'You do know you use Jamie as an excuse to avoid any discussion you don't want to have?'

She sealed her lips and said nothing.

'So this is your plan, to pretend nothing has happened?' he asked, choosing to forget that barely a minute earlier that had been his own plan A.

'Jamie will always come first,' Marisa said, looking away as he swung his legs over the side of the low bed they had shared. The flash fire of desire she felt as his naked body was revealed in all its glory scared her; the complete lack of control she'd just displayed scared her.

And with good reason. She knew from experience that where Roman was concerned she had no pride whatsoever, that when he was in the equation need and desire overrode every moral and practical consideration.

She had finally achieved the safety and stability her life had always lacked. Roman was the antithesis of safe and stable; he was wild and unpredictable… If it had only been her own heart and pride she was gambling with she would've thrown caution to the wind, she would have followed her heart, her instincts.

But this wasn't just about what she wanted, what she *craved*. It couldn't be. She was a mother now, and it wasn't enough to tell her son that she loved him—after all, her own father had loved her. She was determined that Jamie would have the stability that she had always longed for growing up.

Roman was in their lives now, but for how long would that last, especially once he realised how she felt about him? The fact she hadn't blurted out her feelings for him during their recent lovemaking had been luck rather than any caution on her part. If she allowed it to happen again she might not be so lucky next time.

'Should I have a problem with Jamie coming first? I feel the same way,' Roman said.

You can talk the talk, Roman, but can you walk the walk? he thought broodingly. *If you know your son's best interests are best served by taking yourself out of his life, will you do the right thing—will you even recognise what the right thing is? Or will you be blinded by love and even blinder to the damage you inflict in its name?*

He turned his head sharply, his chest heaving with the effort of pushing away the mocking voice of self-doubt in his head as he countered the argument by admitting that he loved his son, but what he felt for Marisa was likely as much to do with the chemistry of dopamine levels in his brain as any deeper romantic connection.

'You...?' She stopped and then redirected her gaze over one of his powerful shoulders, staring off into the distance. 'Will you put some clothes on? I can't concentrate when you're…like that. Just put some clothes on,' she finished lamely.

Pushing free of the battle in his head, he grinned, eliciting an indignant outburst from her.

'Do not look so damned smug!'

His grin did not fade as he walked across to a wooden chest the other side of the daybed. Lifting the lid, he rifled through the folded contents and in moments brought out a pair of swimming shorts and a tee shirt.

'There are swimsuits in there,' she accused.

Pulling the tee shirt over his head, he paused to nod before smoothing down the fabric that clung to the dampness of his skin, moulding it to the corrugated muscles of his belly. 'Some.'

'Why didn't you mention it before?'

'You didn't really give me the chance, did you? You jumped in fully clothed.'

She didn't respond to this vastly modified version of events.

'Why did you marry Rupert?' he suddenly asked.

The shock of the question made Marisa freeze. 'You know why.'

'I know there's something you aren't telling

me, because you wouldn't have the sense to marry for money.'

'Dad's debts were—' She stopped and gave a deep sigh, deciding to tell him everything. She was certain Rupert wouldn't have minded her telling the truth to the father of her child. 'Rupert knew he was dying when he asked me to marry him, Roman, and he had already lost his lover—the love of his life. You see, Rupert was gay. His partner was not out, because he'd been married with a family, and then he died very suddenly. Rupert couldn't even go to his funeral. So he had no one to be with him during his last illness. I think it broke Rupert's heart when his lover died, and his biggest fear was being alone when he died.'

'And so he wasn't,' Roman said softly.

She shook her head. 'No, because I agreed to be his wife, in name only.' Her eyes lifted and there were tears standing out in them. 'He really was a very lovely man. A kind, thoughtful person.'

'He would have made a good father.'

'*You* are Jamie's father.'

'Yes, I am, and...so I've been thinking about Jamie.' Not exclusively, he had to admit, because he had been mostly thinking about how his and Marisa's bodies and desires were so perfectly attuned. How much he wanted her.

At what point did wanting become dangerous?

'Oh?'

He stifled the stab of guilt he felt at what he was about to suggest. He knew he was exploiting her greatest weakness, which was Jamie.

She probably deserved better than he was about to offer.

There was an irony in the acknowledgment when you considered that, to him, for the last few years she had symbolised everything that was treacherous. She had highlighted his weakness, a weakness he hadn't known he had.

He nodded towards the pile of tumbled pillows. 'That was great, I hope you'll agree.'

'I assume you're not asking me for reassurance on your technique, Roman, or a score out of ten.'

'No, but neither am I suggesting marriage.'

Her eyes flew wide. 'I never thought you were,' she said faintly. 'Do you mind telling me what you *are* suggesting?'

'That we become a…team.'

'A team? Is there a uniform? Do we have a coach?'

He frowned at her flippancy. 'Team Jamie, I mean. Because we both want what is best for him—I think we have already established that.'

She nodded.

'What just happened—'

'Can't happen again,' she interjected swiftly.

He looked knowingly at her. 'But we both know that it will. Don't we?'

Her eyes slid from his.

'You are the best sex I have ever had, and we already have a son together so I don't think it would require any great sacrifices for us to work in partnership to ensure the best interests of our child. It will require a few adjustments, but we could divide our time between Spain and England, and I think exclusivity is an obvious—'

His ability to make the outrageous sound normal took Marisa's breath away but she finally managed to speak. 'Let me get this straight. You are offering me exclusive access to your body in exchange for letting you be part of Jamie's life?'

'A bit simplistic but essentially, yes. You have no family, no support network.'

'So you want to be my family, but you also want your freedom. You want to take me to bed but you don't want to take me on a date,' she charged angrily.

'You want to go on a date?'

'Right now I want…' Her eyes slid to the sensual line of his lips and instantly he moved in closer.

'You can have everything you want,' he promised throatily.

But not love, she thought sadly, *not love.*

'I want to be Jamie's dad.'

'I know, but… What if you meet someone else who—'

'I suggest we cross that bridge if we ever come to it.' He arched a brow. 'You're not saying no, so you're thinking about it.'

'Family is about love, not convenience, Roman.'

'I love Jamie.'

She swallowed. 'I know you do,' she admitted, standing there and letting him kiss her.

'We could make this work, Marisa.'

The words were whispered against her mouth.

'What do you say?' Another drugging, persuasive kiss.

'I don't know… We could maybe try…?' she murmured, unable to think straight.

The kiss swept her off her feet and they sank together back onto the cushions of the daybed.

CHAPTER TWELVE

IT HAD BEEN three weeks since they had made love by the pool and so far their unconventional arrangement meant that some of his clothes hung in Marisa's wardrobe and there were two toothbrushes in the bathroom.

Was it enough?

Not nearly but it was all she had.

Would she walk away from it? Did she even want to?

It seemed to Marisa that her life suddenly had a lot more questions than answers. There had been moments when her doubts had become so deafeningly loud that she felt as if her head were exploding, but then she saw Roman and Jamie together, a look, a laugh, a small hand enfolded in a strong one and the noise abated to a soft, bearable murmur of unease.

She glanced at her phone before she slid it back into her pocket. Roman had taken Jamie to visit the stables so that he could give the carrot he'd selected to the pony he had fallen in love with. She had expected them back some time ago, but had they already returned and she'd missed them?

If Jamie had fallen for the pony, he had fallen even harder for his father. Yesterday she had found him sitting alongside Roman in his study, cutely mirroring everything his father did. She decided to try there first before she checked out the stables.

The study was empty but, drawn to the crayon drawing on the desk that Roman had framed, she wandered in to take a closer look. As she picked it up, a smile curving her lips, she hit the corner of the desk and the open laptop wobbled and came to life.

She was about to close the lid when she saw what was on the screen and froze.

An hour later Roman was making his way along the hallway to his study when he saw Marisa coming out of it; she was still in the study when she heard Roman's footsteps in the hallway, her face a mask of grim determination.

'Where's Jamie?' she demanded.

'Were you looking for me?' Roman asked, looking past her through the open doorway she had just appeared through. He was still buzzing with what had just happened outside and he had an idea that he wanted to run past her. An image of the wistful look on Jamie's face as he'd watched two of Maria's brothers playing together appeared in his head. Would Marisa also see the logic in wanting to give Jamie a brother or sister?

Marisa said nothing, just turned and walked back into his office.

'Did you tell Jamie I'm his father?' he asked.

She shook her head and looked confused for a moment.

'Well, he knows.'

She frowned. 'No, that isn't possible.'

'I'm telling you, he knows—I heard one of Maria's brothers ask him if I was his dad and Jamie said yes… The thing is he sounded so casual, like it wasn't even a big deal.' He gave an incredulous laugh and dragged a hand through his hair. 'And we were worrying about when to tell him. I suppose kids hear more than you imagine, and…' His brow furrowed as he registered the tear stains on her pale cheeks, and his concern was immediate. 'What's wrong? Are you all right?'

Hands on her hips, she fixed him with an ice-cold stare. 'I said, where's Jamie?'

Right, so something *was* wrong, very wrong. Roman didn't need to be psychic to see that.

'He's playing with Maria's brothers, the two youngest. He was so thrilled when they invited him to play. It's fine—they can speak enough English to make themselves understood.'

'I need him to come back here now.'

'OK...' he said slowly. 'Maria said she'll fetch him back in time for lunch. Marisa, you should have seen his face when he was watching them play, before they invited him to join them; he looked so wistful. I always had Rio... Do you ever think Jamie's lonely?'

Marisa just stared at him. 'Did you hear what I said?'

'What's the hurry? He's safe and enjoying himself.'

'We are going home!'

His eyes narrowed and without his even moving a muscle his body language made a dramatic shift. When he spoke his voice was flat, his speech slow and deliberate. 'Are you going to tell me what's wrong?'

'Oh, I'm sure *you'll* tell *me*. After all, you already know everything about me, don't you, Roman?' She threw him a look of utter disdain and stalked stiff-backed across to his desk where his laptop lay open. 'I was looking for you when I bumped into the desk. The thing woke up…and can you imagine my surprise when I saw *my* name on the PDF file onscreen?'

As she spoke, a chill spread through his body. He knew before she'd reached the big reveal what had happened. *Dios*, the file was only there because he had intended to delete it and then… He couldn't even remember what had distracted him. The missed call from his mother, maybe—he still hadn't rung her back.

'This isn't what it looks like, Marisa.'

'Oh, you mean you didn't sit there and let me spill my guts to you about my dad's gambling and my mother finding me so lovable that she wiped me out of her life, while already knowing all about it?' Marisa's voice cracked and she had to take a deep breath before she could trust herself to go on. 'You let me open up to you, Roman, when all along you already knew every last tiny detail. There is stuff in that file that even *I* had forgotten.'

She stood there *willing* him to intervene, *willing* him to say something that would put her in the wrong. She so *wanted* to be wrong about this. But his stony expression and the sinking feeling in the pit of her stomach told her she wasn't.

He might not love her, but she had started to believe and respect the fact that he didn't pretend, that he was upfront, and all the time he'd been manipulating her emotions to get what he wanted. Frustration and fear settled over her like a dark fog. She had started to fool herself that they had something beyond the physical and Jamie, but she was wrong.

She had *wanted* to believe that *Team Jamie* was some sort of permanent solution, which only made her look completely sad and pathetic, she concluded.

It begged the question: how many nasty realities was she prepared to turn a blind eye to? Without warning an image of her dad's face floated into her head, his optimistic smile that he had fallen lucky, that he was onto a sure thing that would turn around their fortunes, even though she had been able to see the sadness in his eyes, because he didn't really believe it himself.

Her hunger for security and continuity and Roman's love was, she realised now, as strong as her poor dad's drive to be the big personality, the success story.

The memory of her first instinct when she had seen her name on the open file surfaced. She hadn't closed the laptop or her eyes—but she had really, really wanted to. Would she keep her eyes open the next time…and the next…or one day would she close them? Did she want to live her life with that same desperate fake optimism she had regularly seen in her dad's eyes? And how long would it be before Jamie could see all the lies too?

She squared her shoulders and unconsciously donned a quiet dignity as her eyes found his.

'Have you any idea how it makes me feel,' she said quietly, 'to know that all the time I was opening up to you, you knew? You knew about Dad's debts after he died, the men who threatened me when I couldn't pay the money back, and said I could make things easier on myself by being nice to some of their *friends*. Somehow sleeping my way out of debt didn't feel like such a great option to me. You know, that look on your face really is very convincing,' she admired nastily as the betrayal rising up inside her grabbed her in a vicious chokehold. 'You've got the horrified thing off really well.'

He shook his head, looking more shattered now than shocked, but she refused to be influenced by his superlative acting skills. She'd been fooled by him before.

'It's all there in black and white.' She pointed at the computer screen. 'My life has tabloid headlines written all over it, doesn't it? Maybe one of your Hollywood friends could make it into a movie?'

It took Roman several moments before he could trust himself to speak, to control the images her shocking disclosures had stirred to lurid life in his head. Several more moments to move beyond the protective rage that made him feel nothing was more important than seeking revenge on the animals who had issued the vile threats to her. Ripping the world apart until he found them did not seem at all excessive to him.

A sordid world had touched Marisa but she had emerged untainted. She was, he decided as a surge of cleansing emotion supplanted his anger, the strongest person that he knew.

'I didn't know.' It sounded as pathetic a response as it felt, his brow furrowed as he registered his own outstretched hand. He saw her flinch away and let it fall, acknowledging the knife thrust of pain that her rejection inflicted on him.

Marisa's body was tense, every muscle quivering and taut. She had wanted so much to be able to reach out and be pulled into his body, to pretend that none of this had happened. There was still a shameful part of her that wished she had not confronted him.

'Do you know how all this makes me feel?'

Betrayed, she thought, ruthlessly pushing down the sob in her throat.

'Other than I don't want to be in the same room as you?'

She saw his nostrils flare as he inhaled sharply as if she had struck him, and told herself she didn't care. She wanted him to hurt, because he had hurt her; he had *betrayed* her trust.

'I've never told anyone about my mum and her *other* family either, not even Dad. He never knew that she had remarried, and that her so-cial-media accounts are full of photos of her great, talented stepsons and her lovely daugh-ter—my half-sister.

'Turns out, you see, that it wasn't mother-hood she couldn't cut, it was *me*. And to es-cape me she ran all the way to America, where she has a lovely family she dotes on, bakes cakes for the church fetes and fundraisers for the local school. But, yet again, I'm only tell-ing you what you already know—*aren't I?*'

'I am so sorry, Marisa,' Roman said, ach-ing for her pain, seeing vividly the little girl who had lived with the worst possible rejection grow up only for it to happen all over again. 'If I had known—'

What, Roman? What would you have done? Protected her!

The thing she needs protecting from is you! sneered the unrelenting voice of disdain in his head.

'Do not *dare* say that,' she hissed through

clenched teeth. 'And don't dare to act as if this is all news to you. You already know every-thing about me, whether I've chosen to tell you or not.'

'I know you're the bravest, kindest, warm-est, strongest person I know.'

And I love you, he thought desperately as the self-deception he had clung to like a lifeline finally slipped through his exhausted grip like wet rope. Maintaining that deception had been such a struggle, but letting it go came without relief because along with it went the protec-tion it had afforded.

While he had been able to deflect and think only of chemistry, sex, passion—anything but love—he had been able to tell himself that this situation was manageable, desirable even.

People spent their lives looking for love, but he had spent his life avoiding it, knowing better than most the dangerous, destructive powers of living with such an all-consuming obsessive passion.

The sincerity in his voice as he'd listed her qualities had clearly only made her angrier than ever. She gave a shudder of disgust and held up her hand as he surged towards her, his hands outstretched. 'No!'

He stopped at her command, his hands falling to his sides once more, his face a mask of pain.

He saw the hurt, the pain, the utter rejection in her face and felt his heart sink. Was she right to hold him off? True, he hadn't done what she'd imagined, he'd never read that extended report on her, but he was capable of doing a lot worse, he knew that. He was never going to be a positive influence in her life or Jamie's.

How could he be? He was far too flawed. His father had not set out to hurt him, but the end result was the same and he was his father's son, wasn't he? It was a fact and a fate that he could not escape.

His father had crushed his mother with his love, instead of setting her free. The idea of inflicting that sort of pain on Marisa and their son was too painful for Roman to contemplate.

In one way at least he could prove that he was not his father's son, that he was better than that, or at the very least possessed some self-awareness of the damage he could do.

The cost…the price…would be high but the only way he could prove his love for Marisa and Jamie was to let them go.

It was something he knew he had to do before his selfish instincts, the ones that were screaming at him to keep them close, drowned out his better self.

'I'm sorry.'

It was subtle, almost imperceptible, but the change, the *something* in his manner brought a defensive stiffness to Marisa's attitude. She found herself bracing herself for something—though the *what* remained elusive.

'I think you're right, this isn't working,' he said.

She knew this, she'd been screaming for him to recognise this, so why did hearing him confirm what she already knew feel as though someone had just kicked her in the stomach?

'So what…?'

'If you want to go home I'm not going to stop you.'

She took a deep breath, and refused to flinch as his words and their meaning hit painfully home. She passed a hand across her eyes as she blinked away tears of anger and humiliation. This was one occasion when she didn't want to be proved right.

It didn't matter that she'd been planning to walk through the door anyway. It was, she discovered, an infinitely more humiliating thing entirely to have it held open for you as you went.

'I never needed your permission,' she flared back before, a moment later, her haughtiness morphed into bitterness. 'So you got bored with being a father after all.' It was as if he'd just decided the hassle was all too much trouble, easier by far to walk away. Only better still, he didn't have to because this was his home and she was the one walking away from him.

Something flashed in his dark eyes, but a moment later it was gone. His voice was flat and even as he said quietly, 'I'll make sure the jet is available.'

Pride was the only thing stopping her falling down as he walked away. The moment he vanished so did her defiance, but she was robbed of the release of tears because Jamie arrived smelling of the stables and demanding she come with him so he could show her the correct way to groom a horse.

The *castillo* had never felt this empty before.

Roman had locked himself in his study and sat looking at a decanter of brandy, although his glass remained empty. He knew it wouldn't help because it would take a lot more than alcohol to dull the pain, the emptiness inside him.

The first time his mobile rang he ignored it. The second time he intended to do the same, then with a sudden intake of breath he reached for the offending instrument. What if it was Marisa and she needed him? It was amazing how many nightmare scenarios a man could imagine in between grabbing a phone and ramming it to his ear.

'Roman, my, you are a difficult man to get hold of.'

His shoulders sagged. 'Mother.'

'So glad you recognise my voice after all this time and, before you say it, I know I wasn't very welcoming the last time you saw me, but hospitals really do not bring out the best in me. I wanted to tell you that I am back home now after what I hope will be my last surgery. Everything went well and I'm planning to visit my granddaughter shortly. I thought you could possibly join me at the beach house? You have no idea how happy I am that at least one of you is settled. I was always worried about Rio.'

'Why Rio?' Roman asked, pretending an interest he didn't feel as he reached for the decanter and filled the glass. It might not help but he was now working on the theory that it could surely not make things any worse.

'I know I'm being silly, but he could just be so possessive as a child and, when he was angry, he had a way of holding his head that occasionally made me think of... But of course, he is nothing like your father.'

Roman placed the glass down with a bang that sloshed the contents over the polished surface. 'Rio, like Father?' He had to have misheard.

'I know... I know, so stupid of me. You are both your own men, and you always were.'

'Rio?'

'Are you all right, Roman?'

'People used to say that *I* was like Father.'

His mother's merry laughter echoed down

the line. 'What people?' she scoffed. 'Heavens, are you serious? *You?*

'You are *nothing* like your father at all. In fact, you are the total antithesis of him, which is why I never worried about you as much as I did Rio. You are moody and emotional, and your father was a very cold and calculating man. Oh, he spoke a lot about love, but the truth was he was incapable of feeling the emotion, because he was all about control and revenge. The only thing you inherited from your father was your head for business! Roman, are you still there?'

'Yes, Mother, but I have to go now.'

Could it be true?

Was it possible that he was so afraid of becoming the very thing he'd most despised and feared, he had created a scenario that did not exist, and he had seen monsters in him that were not there?

He picked up the framed drawing from the desk before the spreading brandy reached it, and stared at the childish drawing, feeling as if his heart would burst.

He ached for Marisa.

He ached for their son too, yet his suffering

was of his own making. He'd thought he was being noble, doing the right thing for them... but what if all he was actually being was a coward?

He had sent them away! A sound of disgust was wrenched from his throat. He was sitting here alone, being a martyr, when actually he was simply a fool—a coward and a fool.

A sense of calm settled over him as he brushed the mess off the desk with his forearm and placed the picture back carefully centre stage, which was where his family should be.

He reached for his phone to call his pilot.

'Santiago, I have a favour to ask.'

The 'staying cheerful' thing was taking its toll. Marisa already felt exhausted after a journey from hell to the private airport, during which Jamie had loudly demanded to take his pony and Roman, not necessarily in that order, back home with him.

All she wanted to do was curl up in a corner and cry, but crying was not a luxury that mums always had.

And now, just when she'd thought the worst was over, the flight, for some reason that was too technical for her to grasp, was delayed. At least they were delayed in luxury and the on-board staff were keeping Jamie amused playing games. She glanced towards her son, who was crying out, 'I win, I win,' after he had carefully counted out six on the dice.

'Excuse me.'

She turned to see the pilot standing beside her.

'Not more delay?' She sighed.

'Everything is moving along nicely,' he soothed. 'But there is an issue with some of the luggage. If you could just come outside for a moment?'

'Luggage?'

He shrugged and smiled. 'These officials can be persistent.'

Which told her nothing at all. She glanced over at Jamie.

'He'll be fine. I'll keep an eye on him myself.'

She recognised the sleek supercar before she even saw the driver.

'Hello, Marisa.'

She spun around, her blonde hair flying around her face. Brushing the shiny strands from her face gave her time to think, except of course she couldn't. Thoughts were firing off at wild tangents in her head, not making any sense, the processes of logic completely overwhelmed by the surge of raw emotion that blocked out everything else... There was just her heartbeat and the sensation of deep longing.

'I like your hair loose.' His caressing glance drifted over her pale hair before coming to rest on her face, his own settling into an expression that hinted at an aching loneliness inside him.

She cleared her throat and looked away, refusing to see things that were not there. She had to deal with the real world, not fantasies, which were lovely while they lasted but so, so painful when you woke up.

'What are you doing here, Roman?'

Her chin lifted as she added silently, *Besides compounding my misery.* She hadn't asked to fall in love but she had, and as she looked up at his perfectly gorgeous face she could not imagine a time when he did not make her ache with longing.

With a tiny groan she squeezed her eyes

closed and begged huskily, 'Will you just go away and leave me in peace?'

'No.'

Her eyes opened in response to the thumb under her chin.

He was there standing right in front of her, his body blocking out everything else, but then when he was around there was nothing else for her to see.

'Not yet.' His lips were warm as they moved across her own. 'Not ever,' he added on a throaty murmur as he kissed her again, this time with a ferocity that matched the possessive intent etched on his dark features.

Hands clenched at her sides, she fought against the surge of passion that made her want to cling to him, and with a small cry she stepped backwards, her pallor highlighted by the two patches of colour on her cheeks as she panted like someone who had just run a marathon.

'What is this all about, Roman? Because...' She glanced at the stationary jet, its metallic paint glinting in the sun. 'You arranged this delay, didn't you?'

'Yes. I needed to talk to you.'

She touched her lips. 'That wasn't talking.'

Roman sketched a smile that did not reach his dark eyes, which remained desperate and determined. 'Your mouth always distracts me. The *castillo* felt empty when you left.'

Empty, sterile, safe…*very* safe—just like his life. People called him reckless and a risk-taker when he pitted himself against an unclimbable peak, but he wasn't a risk-taker, he was a coward, he thought with a fresh surge of self-contempt. What he was about to do, now *that* was real risk-taking.

Giving something of himself.

The cost of moving on was high, but he needed to let her see him as he really was.

'Yes, I did order that dossier on you to be compiled, but I hadn't ever opened it. I had no idea what was in it until you told me.'

She planted her hands on her hips, an effect spoilt by the fact she had to brush away the tears that were trickling down her cheeks. 'You've driven all this way just to tell me that? You expect me to *believe* you?'

'No, but it happens to be true.' His chest lifted in a deep sigh. His future, his soul depended on him convincing her.

'I had every intention of deleting it from my computer, I really did.'

'Because you were not interested in my skeletons,' she said dryly.

'I'm interested in *everything* about you,' he said honestly. 'And I was very tempted to access that material, but I didn't because... I think I wanted you to tell me yourself, when you were ready.'

'Because you are *so* patient.'

He conceded her jab with a shrug. 'Maybe it was arrogant of me, but I wanted you to trust me.' His lips quirked in a bitter little smile. '*Dios*, this is not easy.'

'And flying away from you is?' she yelled back.

'Then don't go,' he pushed out fiercely through clenched teeth before continuing in the same driven tone. 'I wanted, I *needed* you to trust me enough to tell me. I genuinely had no idea about your mother and half-sister until you told me. For the record, it is not your fault, it is hers, and not having you in her life is definitely her loss. I am speaking here as someone who has lost you once and, while I am so glad Rupert was there to save you, I just wish it had been me instead, *mi vida*.'

She blinked and he took encouragement from the doubt that he saw creep into her golden eyes.

'I don't believe you.' But he didn't think she sounded completely sure and he pressed home the only advantage he had left.

'It is true. What is also true is that I love you. You are the only woman in the world I have ever said that to. The last time you threw it back in my face and walked away with a chunk of me that I've never got back.'

She took a step towards him, her eyes scanning his face. 'You love me...?'

'From that very first moment I saw you.'

She looked utterly shocked.

'I have always been afraid that if I let myself care about someone, allowed myself to fall in love, I would become just like him and destroy the very thing that I loved most.'

'Your father?'

He nodded. 'The anger, the rage inside me when you told me you were already married... it was...' He closed his eyes, the sinews in his neck standing out as he fought against the tidal wave of black memories. 'I walked away from my life, and I rebuilt those walls you knocked down around my heart, but I added a few more feet for good measure, as much to keep my anger in as to keep love out. I shouldn't be telling you this.'

'You *should* be telling me,' Marisa contradicted, stepping in and framing his face with loving hands and sharing a watery smile when he opened his eyes.

'You believe me.'

'I do.' She felt lighter for just saying it. 'I love you, Roman, so much it scares me, because loving you feels like I'm stepping into moving traffic with my eyes closed.' She gave a wild little laugh. 'They say the best cure for fears and secrets is fresh air. You can't keep everything in, and I can't any more,' she admitted.

'If it ever gets too heavy for you to bear, you need to share—you need to share with me. You really are incredible, you know.' Unable to resist the soft invitation of her lips, he kissed her with a tenderness bordering on reverence.

'You'll make me cry,' she warned thickly.

'If I ever hurt you, Marisa, it would kill me—' he groaned out fiercely.

'You are *nothing* like him,' she cut in fiercely. 'Do you hear me, Roman Bardales? Nothing! There is a massive difference between wanting to *protect* someone because you love them and wanting to *control* them because you don't know what love really is. You love our son and I know that you will always protect him. That makes me feel...safe. You make me feel safe.'

'Marisa.' He swallowed, his voice cracking with emotion as he stroked a finger down her smooth cheek.

'I want to be Superman for our son.'

'He doesn't need a superhero, he just needs a dad. He needs you.' Her lashes dipped over her eyes as she gazed at him through them. 'We both do, Roman.'

'You have me, you have had me from that moment in the rain when you looked up at me and the rest of the world went away.'

'You and Jamie are my entire world,' she whispered against his mouth.

He sighed in contentment. 'Let's go home.'

EPILOGUE

'WHY ARE WE HERE? I have a table at the restaurant booked for—' Roman turned his wrist, pushed up the cuff of the fine black cashmere sweater he wore over black jeans and glanced at the metal-banded watch '—half an hour ago.' He sighed. The famous Michelin-starred restaurant was the only thing that would normally have made the journey to this quiet south coast seaside town worthwhile.

When he had acquiesced to Marisa's surprise request to spend the weekend here he had assumed that the place had some special significance for her, maybe from childhood, but no, she seemed as unfamiliar with the place as he was.

The mystery remained but he was content to let it play out.

'I am not dressed for the beach.' He looked around at the empty stretch of sand lined with beach huts, but it did not surprise him it was empty; the wind was blowing up a positive sandstorm. 'Sand gets everywhere.'

'Don't be such a grouch,' she retorted. 'We are nearly there.' She was studying the brightly painted beach huts they were passing and was, he realised, counting under her breath. 'This is it!' she exclaimed.

He shook his head. He could see someone jogging along a deserted promenade and a dog walker who was a mere dot in the distance.

'You have bought me a beach hut?'

It was a joke, but then she went to knock on the door of the candy-striped wooden box they were standing beside.

'Marisa!'

She shook her head, suddenly looking nervous. 'You will thank me, I promise you,' she said, sounding as if she was trying to convince herself. She tapped on the door, which opened immediately.

A slim figure wearing large sunglasses and a loose hooded sweat top that concealed her hair stepped out, nodding at Marisa, who turned to him with a plea in her golden eyes.

'Just please go inside, Roman, and then you'll understand.'

He would have stepped inside a burning building if she had asked him, so this request did not require much thought. He ducked to go through the door and heard a key click in the lock behind him.

'I'll come back for you in half an hour!' Marisa yelled through the door.

As he had already seen through the disguise of the woman in the hoodie he was not surprised by the identity of the solo occupant of the beach hut, who was sitting on an unfolded deckchair.

The figure got to his feet. 'It would seem you are late.'

'If I'd known where I was going, I wouldn't be here at all,' Roman said, staring with distaste around the hut's interior, lit by a single bulb suspended from the ceiling. 'I am assuming that we are meant to sort out our differences in half an hour, and then emerge as friends?'

'That appears,' Rio agreed dryly, 'to be the general idea. Or I could even the scales and put you on the floor this time,' he added, rubbing his clean-shaven jaw.

'You could try,' Roman retorted.

KIM LAWRENCE 279

The brothers stood staring at one another for a moment, then in unison they grinned and, stepping forward into one another, embraced.

'So who do you suppose had this cunning little idea?' Rio asked. 'Gwen or Marisa?'

'I think I know when they made contact, because a couple of weeks ago Marisa was looking *really* guilty.'

Rio nodded. 'Yes, that time frame works for my end too,' he admitted with a laugh. 'Well, are we going to tell them this little charade was not actually necessary, that we'd already met, shook hands and made up?'

'How about we leave them thinking they have knocked our stubborn heads together and saved the day?'

Rio grinned. 'Shall we throw a few things around too to make it look authentic?'

'What is this place anyway?'

'I think we might find our other halves bid for it in an online auction—but it could have been worse,' Rio said.

'How so?'

'They could be leaving us in here for an hour.'

Roman laughed. 'And in the meantime do

you have those dates?' he asked, digging in a pocket for his phone.

'You spoke to Mum?'

Roman nodded. 'She is willing to come back to the *castillo* for the big day, as long as she can bring her significant other.'

'He really is all right, you know.'

'So long as he makes her happy,' Roman said simply.

'Wow, you really have changed your tune—is that Marisa's influence?'

Roman slung him a look. 'So the venue is sorted, it's just a matter of when suits us all.'

'The sooner the better, as far as I'm concerned...' Rio paused. 'Before Gwen starts showing.'

Roman's eyes widened. 'Congratulations... I don't suppose that this is a spring baby?'

'End of—' Rio stopped dead. *'You too?'*

Roman nodded, looking proud. 'Well, not me personally, but Marisa found out last week. Jamie is going to have a brother or sister, maybe both if we're really lucky.'

'Twins?' Rio released a low chuckle. 'This is going to be one hell of a wedding, brother, in a good way.'

'I have a feeling it's going to be one hell of a life, in the very best way,' Roman countered.

Not just a society wedding, but a *joint* wedding of the most eligible bachelors in Europe, held in the incredible setting of the Bardales estate.

The world's media only had one complaint: that they were not allowed inside. The rich and famous were invited and, so it was said, most of the locals for miles around too. They took comfort in the knowledge that someone would have smuggled in a phone, that *someone* would be tempted by a fat wedge of cash.

They would get their story.

What they did get was a snapshot made publicly available that showed both couples sitting on a bale of hay looking happy, and the world's media spent a full week furiously speculating on who was responsible for this naturalistic shot.

A week later, sprawled on the cushions of the daybed beside his wife, Roman watched Jamie swim-splashing in the new addition to the landscaping, a baby pool filled with inflatable toys, while he read aloud an article in the paper.

'"It seems that the truth is out: the wedding photo, it has been definitively decided, was taken by famous photographer Sir Robert Chambers, who is refusing to confirm the rumours, but a source close to him apparently says"—'

A protective hand on the gentle swell of her belly, Marisa broke into peels of musical laughter.

'Imagine,' Roman said, leaning over to remove her hand and kiss the small bump before he placed it back and covered the pale fingers with his own big hand. 'If our son has a talent worthy of such a towering artistic icon at only four.'

'Five next,' Marisa corrected with a grin.

'Five next, but imagine what he will be capable of by the time he is eighteen.'

'If he is anything like his father, he'll be breaking hearts, I would think.'

Roman caught her hand and pulled Marisa against him. 'There is only one heart I am interested in,' he husked, curving a possessive hand over the curve of her left breast, 'and I do not want to break it. I want to love it like I do every single part of you.' He placed a gentle kiss on her mouth.

'Well, soon there'll be a lot more of me to love than there was, so you'd better leave plenty of time,' she retorted against his warm lips.

'Time is not a problem. We have the rest of our lives.'

With a sigh Marisa allowed herself to be drawn into his arms and Roman held her tight. He never wanted to let her go.

He wasn't aware he had spoken aloud until Marisa whispered back, 'Don't even try to let me go, Bardales. I'm a keeper.'

* * * * *

LET'S TALK
Romance

For exclusive extracts, competitions
and special offers, find us online:

f facebook.com/millsandboon

⊙ @millsandboonuk

𝕏 @millsandboon

Or get in touch on 0844 844 1351*

For all the latest titles coming soon,
visit millsandboon.co.uk/nextmonth

*Calls cost 7p per minute plus your phone company's price per
minute access charge